Mr. Foote

A Trip to Calais

A Comedy in Three Acts

Mr. Foote

A Trip to Calais
A Comedy in Three Acts

ISBN/EAN: 9783744785020

Printed in Europe, USA, Canada, Australia, Japan

Cover: Foto ©Andreas Hilbeck / pixelio.de

More available books at **www.hansebooks.com**

A

TRIP TO CALAIS;

AND THE

CAPUCHIN.

WRITTEN by Mr. FOOTE,

PUBLISHED by Mr. COLMAN.

[Price Two Shillings and Six-pence.]

A

TRIP TO CALAIS;

A Comedy in Three Acts.

AS ORIGINALLY WRITTEN,

AND INTENDED FOR REPRESENTATION,

By the late SAMUEL FOOTE, Esq.

To which is annexed,

THE

CAPUCHIN;

AS IT IS PERFORMED AT THE

THEATRE-ROYAL in the HAYMARKET.

ALTERED FROM THE

TRIP TO CALAIS,

BY THE LATE

SAMUEL FOOTE, Esq.

AND NOW PUBLISHED BY

Mr. COLMAN.

LONDON,
Printed by T. Sherlock,
For T. CADELL, in the Strand.

MDCCLXXVIII.

ADVERTISEMENT.

THAT the Publick may not be deceived, and the Reputation of the Author injured, by the publication of Pieces, fabricated in order to take an undue advantage of the general curiofity, the Comedy of A TRIP TO CALAIS is here printed, as originally written, and intended for reprefentation; together with all the Alterations and Additions which the Writer thought neceffary, when he afterwards produced it on the ftage, under the title of THE CAPUCHIN.

DRAMATIS

DRAMATIS PERSONÆ.

Colonel CROSBY.
O'DONNOVAN.
MINNIKIN.
KIT CODLING.
DICK DRUGGET.
LUKE LAPELLE.
GREGORY GINGHAM.
TROMFORT.
KIT CABLE.
LA JEUNESSE.
SERVANT.

Soldiers, Porters, Shoe-Blacks, &c.

Lady KITTY CROCODILE.
Miſs LYDELL.
Mrs. MINNIKIN.
Mrs. CLACK.
JENNY MINNIKIN.
HETTY.
ABBESS.
NUN.

A

TRIP TO CALAIS.

ACT I.

Scene, Hotel d'Angleterre.

Enter Kit Cable, Dick Drugget, and Jenny Minnikin.

Cable.

HARKEE, meſſmate! look about! you had better bring-to in this creek: Here you will find the beſt moorings. The *Hotel d'Angleterre* they calls it in French; but you'll find the names of things plaguily tranſmogrified all along this coaſt. •

Dick. They be civil people, no doubt.

Cable. Civil? ay, ay; if you will bring a good cargo of caſh, you are welcome to anchor here as long as you liſt: But you will find the duties high at out-clearance; therefore take

B   care,

care, d'ye fee, and don't run aground.   I muft
take t'other trip to the port, for your ftowage.

[*Exit.*

Dick. J hope by this time your fea-ficknefs is
pretty well gone ?

Jenny. Much mended, dear Dicky, I thank
you.

Dick. Well, my dear Jenny, here we are,
fafely landed in the French country, however.
And now, what's next to be done ? Confider,
my love, we have not a moment to lofe ; your
father will not be long behind us, I am fure.

Jenny. No queftion of that ; therefore our beft
way will be to get out of his power as foon as
we can.

Dick. By what means ?

Jenny. By the means which we came hither in
fearch of; by being married, you know.

Dick. True : But how the deuce fhall we
procure a parfon ? Perhaps the man of the houfe
may affift us : But, plague on't ! I can't *parley
Françee*; tho' I underftand a few words here and
there.

Jenny. But I can, Dicky, you know.   What,
do you think I was five years at madam Van-
flopping's, the Swifs French boarding-fchool at
Edmonton, for nothing at all ?

· *Dick.* True, true ; I had forgot.—But I don't

think

think it any mark of their manners, to let us wait here so long without asking us in. Here, house, house!

Jenny. Peace, Dicky! how is it possible they should know what you want?—*Maison! seignior de Terre!*

Dick. Who? what?

Jenny. Seignior de Terre is as much as to say Landlord in English.

Dick. True, true. Oh! here the man comes.

Enter Monsieur Tromfort.

Tromf. Monsieur! Mademoiselle!

Dick. To him, Jenny!

Jenny. Monsieur, nos sommes Anglois, & nous avons grand occasion d'un pretre!

Tromf. A quoi faire?

Jenny. Faire? pour nous joindre lui & moi ensemble, I think.

Dick. That is marriage, she and me: You understand me, Mounseer?

Tromf. Ah-ha! *pour le mariage! tres bien;* perfectly vell, Sir.

Dick. Gad's my life, he speaks English! how lucky we were in the choice of a house!—And what may your name be, Mounseer?

Tromf. Tromfort, at your ver good service.

Dick. Why, look'ee! Mounseer Tromfort; in
a word,

a word, our bufinefs is this: This here young
gentlewoman and I——

Jenny. Stop, Dicky, and let me explain matters to MonfieurTromfórt; becaufe why, I fpeak
the language, you know.

Dick. But, Mifs, our landlord underftands
Englifh.

Jenny. No matter; don't contradiét me,
Dicky; you know I could not never bear that
from a child. You muft know then, Monfieur,
that Mr. Matthew Minnikin, my father, is one
of the moft refpeétable pin-makers in the whole
city of London; and that I am his daughter.

Tromf. Ah-ha! I underftand; maifter Minicky, *gros marchand d'epingle? c'eft tout*
fimple.

Jenny. And this here young man that you fee,
is Dicky Drugget, father's 'prentice at home.

Tromf. Fort bien; ver vell!

Jenny. Now, father being minded to provide
me a hufband, for fear I fhould otherwife provide one for myfelf——

Tromf. Fort bien! dat vas ver vell fancy:
Pardie, monfieur Minicky has great deal of
wit!

Jenny. Yes, well enough; if fo be that he had
got me a man to my mind; but he was fo un-
dutiful as never to think of confulting of me.

Tromf.

Tromf. Oh, fy, fy, Monfieur Minicky! dat vas terrible ting.

Jenny. Ay, was it not, Monfieur? quite mon-ftrous, as a body may fay; and fo you would own, if you was to fee the creature he fix'd on: Kit Codling, a fat fifhmonger, hard by the 'Change. They fay the man is well enough to pafs in the world; one of the livery, a pretty good fpeechefyer, minds his fhop, and is careful and fober; but, Lord, what fignifies that? he has no more idera of drefs than a Dutchman; and as to cotillions, I fuppofe he knows as much about them as a cow.

Tromf. Oh, fy, fy! *Mauvaife partie,* bad partie!

Jenny. And fo, Dicky and I being bred up together, as it were, and being a genteelifh vir-tuous young man——

Tromf. Ah, vas *tres gentile.*

Jenny. Yes; for except lying out all night now and then, hating to be fo vulgar as to ftay in the fhop, frequenting the tavern in fearch of good company, running his father in debt for his credit, and gracing his converfation with the oaths moft in fafhion, I don't believe the lad has a fingle vice in the world.

Tromf. Dat is ver extraordinary!

Jenny. And yet you can't think what an ora-
tioning

tioning father us'd to make every day : But, between you and I, Monſieur, father and mother are but a couple of fogrum old fools ; ben't they, Dicky ?

Dick. To ſay truth, little better, my dear.

Jenny. Why, what a noiſe they made about my only running from ſchool for three or four days with Monſieur Chaſſon, our *maitre de dance,* juſt as if they thought I would never come back again ; ha, ha !

Dick. To ſay truth, Mounſeer, Miſs Jenny amongſt them had but a very bad time ; for this I muſt confeſs to her face, ſhe is the moſt beſt-temper'deſt girl in the world ; for let her but ſay and do what ſhe pleaſes, and you will ſcarcely hear a croſs word come out of her mouth in a month.

Tromf. Vraiment ?

Dick. Then, to prove what a dutiful daughter ſhe always has been, ſhe conſtantly uſed to ſteal out to ſee Breſlaw, the plays, and hear Signiora Gamberbelly at the opera, on purpoſe to prevent their being tired with her company at home.

Tromf. Ver conſiderate !

Dick. And whenever the old folks charg'd her with doing any thing wrong, ſhe never told them a word of truth in her life.

Tromf.

Tromf. No?

Dick. No; for fear of making her parents uneafy.

Tromf. Ver *aimable* indeed!

Jenny. Nay, Monfieur, Dicky was always very partial to me.—And fo, we taking a fancy to one another, and to prevent father from expofing himfelf by fuch a ridiculous choice as Kit Codling, we agreed to give the old ones the flip, and take a little tour to the kingdom of France.

Tromf. *Bien imaginée!* dat vas vell imagin!

Dick. And fo, Mounfeer——

Jenny. Nay, Dicky, don't interrupt me, my dear!—And fo, as I was a-faying, if you can contrive to procure us a marrying doctor, for I am told there are one or two who have fet up in that way in this town, we fhall take it, Monfieur, as a very particular favour.

Tromf. I fhall be ver happy, *tres charmée!* to be capable to ferve-a you.

Jenny. Vaft polite! and indeed, as I have often told Dicky, the French always are fo.

Tromf. Indeed, I have great regard for de Englis; and ven dey come over, I never refufe my protection.

Jenny. Mighty civil, indeed!

Tromf. Why, every fummer dere come here

to my houfe a great many my lors; and I let
'em ftay two, tree months, juft as long as dey
pleafe.

Dick. What, for nothing, Mounfeer?

Tromf. Prefque la meme chofe! almoft de very
fame ting; dey never pay noding at all, only
juft for dere eating, drinking, and fleeping.

Jenny. How generous and noble!

Tromf. Yes; I alvays have great *penchant,*
great partiality, for dofe of your country. Vy,
dere vas fome time ago, ven my houfe and
my good vas burn down by de fire, I never vas
take noding at all from de French.

Dick. No?

Tromf. Pas une fous; but fuffer my lors Anglois to build-a my hotel up again to dere own
tafte, vidout de leaft interruption.

Dick. How kind, to give that preference to us!

Jenny. That indeed was the very excefs of
good breeding!

Tromf. And ven dey bring over good many
guinea, lumb'ring heavy great ting, I make de
change vid de louis, dat vas fo pretty, and as
light as de cork.

Jenny. How difinterefted!

Tromf. And as I know Meffieurs les Anglois
come here to improve demfelves by travel in
France, I advife dem always to ftay here as
                                              long

long as dey can, and never to tink of going home, till all dere monies be gone.

Dick. What a fine thing it is to get fuch a friend in foreign parts!

Jenny. True, Dicky. Well, but, Monfieur, do you think you can provide us with the party we want?

Tromf. Pour la mariage? for marry you? dere is no doubt.

Dick. But there is no time, Mounfeer, to be loft, for we expect Mifs's father and mother to follow us in the very firft fhip.

Tromf. Dere is de Doctor Coupler live juft-a by, in de very next ftreet.

Jenny. Then fend for him directly.

Tromf. Very probable he is not at home at dis time.

Dick. No?

Tromf. He commonly take de opportunity of defe dark night, to ftep crofs de Shannel, and fupply his friend on t'oder fide vid de brandy and tea.

Dick. Oh, what, I reckon, the Doctor fmuggles a little?

Tromf. Yes, for little amufement, juft *pour paffer le temps*; for he is ver fond of de fea.

Diek. Will you enquire, Mounfeer, if we cannot meet with the Doctor?

Tromf. A *l'inftant*; dis very moment.

C

Enter

Enter a very old Waiter.

Eh bien? La Jeuneſſe! vat is de matter?

La Jeu. Dere is anoder veſſel from Dover, juſt-a put into de port.

Dick. Is there? Then ten to one your father is in her!

Tromf. Dat vill be ver *mal-à-propos!*

Dick. Hadn't I better run down to the key, and take a peep at who lands.

Tromf. By all mean; de very beſt dought in de vorld.

Dick. Stay you here, Miſs; I will be back in a trice.   [*Exit.*

Tromf. A ver pretty gentleman, dat Maiſter Druggy!

Jenny. Yes, Dicky is thought very well on.

Tromf. He has ver great head; *beaucoup de politique!*

Jenny. Yes, yes; he has wit enough when he will.

Tromf. Ma foi, Maiſter Dicky be *fort!* a ver happy man, to be ſure!

Jenny. How ſo, Monſieur Tromfort?

Tromf. How ſo? *pardie,* to have engage de affection of ſo *aimable* a Mademoiſelle.

Jenny. Dear me, Monſieur, and d'ye think ſo?

Tromf. Aſſurement.

Jenny. Really? But you French are ſo given to flattery!

                                        Tromf.

Tromf. Point de tout, not at all ! Vill you permit-a me, Mademoiſelle, juſt to have de honour to kiſs-a your hand ?

Jenny. My hand, Monſieur ? what good can that do you ?

Tromf. Ah! my God! how fine! vite as ſnow, and ſoft as de ſilk ! Vat vould I give to be dat dere Monſieur Dicky !

Jenny. Why, is it poſſible, Monſieur, that you can think me equal to your own country ladies?

Tromf. Ah, Mademoiſelle, dere is no comparifon at all in de vorld : Vat havock your charm vould make in dis contry !

Jenny. I am not quite ſo certain of that.

Tromf. Dere is no doubt at all : *Pour la preuve*; De very firſt-a Frenchmans you vas ſee, is proud to drow himſelf at your feet.

Jenny. At mine ? who can that be, Monſieur?

Tromf. Votre tres humble, Mademoiſelle; it is *moi*, me myſelf.

Jenny. You ?

Tromf. Moi. Permit-a me, Mademoiſelle, to declare de force of my paſſion, dat burn my ver—

Jenny. For me ? why, I have ſcarce been in your company a couple of minutes.

Tromf. Von inſtant is enough for your charm to make-a de conqueſt; de very firſt glance, your bright eyes ſhoot me quite to de heart. Ah !

C 2   how

how it make-a me pat, pat, pat, pat! *Fait moi l' honneur* to place-a your hand juft here a my fide.

Jenny. Here is an audacious old fop! I'll try how far the impudent puppy will go.—Why, really, Monfieur, you're fo amiable, and your manners fo very polite, and fo civil, that if it had not been for a prior engagement, I don't know but I might be tempted to liften.

Tromf. Courage, Monfieur Tromfort! Stay but littel time, Maifter Dicky, begar I make you a cocu before you vas marry. [*afide.*]—Engagement! vat is dat?

Jenny. The young man you faw here but now.

Tromf. Maifter Dicky; ver vell?

Jenny. We are come over hither to marry, you know.

Tromf. Vy not?

Jenny. What, and at the fame time encourage another's addreffes?

Tromf. To be fure. *En France*, de lady alvays take de hufband to make fure of de lover; de one *pour la politique*, de oder for de paffion.

Jenny. Ay; but what would my countrywomen fay at fo very quick a——

Jenny. Say? ah-ha! fhe begin to capitulate. [*afide.*]—Say? dat you take de ver vife ftep. Oh, Mademoifelle, dere be many pretty my lady who vait at my hotel for de vind, dat can tell many comic ftorie of Monfieur Tromfort.

Jenny.

Jenny. Oh, I don't doubt it at all!—Was there ever fuch an impudent coxcomb!—If one did but know, indeed, the name of fome of the ladies, it would be a kind of excufe.

Tromf. Pardonnez moi! jamais de man of honour; never tell de name of de lady. *La voies!* looky here! look at dis *plumet*; dis pretty white fedder [*fhews a fhably white feather*]; dis trophy of my victory I receive from de hand of de pretty my lady.

Jenny. That indeed is a proof; and yet, Monfieur, it is a fort of wonder too, for you are not over young, nor, between ourfelves, remarkably handfome; and befides all that, you have but one eye.

Tromf. Dat is true; but den confider, Mademoifelle, dat de little god Cupid has got hever a vone.

Jenny. Right; and I believe the lady muft have been near as blind as the god.

Tromf. Not at all. But, *ma chere* Mademoifelle, we lofe time; and Maifter Dicky may come back from de port. Dere is, in dis littel room, de ver pritt picter, which permit-a me to have de honour to fhew you.

Jenny. Nay, but, Monfieur——

Tromf. Dere muft be a littel compulfion to make de lady do vat fhe like [*pulls her.*] *Venez ma!*

Jenny.

Jenny. Hands off, you infolent ruffian!

[*Strikes him.*

Tromf. Diable!

Jenny. The vanity and impudence of this fellow exceeds all the accounts I have heard of his country.

Tromf. By gar, for de foft hand, it is de moft hard I ever vas feel!

Jenny. Not half fo much as you merit. A pretty account you give of the Englifh; and a fine return for all the favours you have received at their hands!

Tromf. Pardie, c'eft une efpèce de virago.—Mais, Mademoifelle!

Jenny. However, the gentleman will foon be back, and return you thanks for this piece of civility.

Tromf. Mais, Mademoifelle, you vas know de mode of dis country, de littel gallantry to de pretty fine vomans.

Jenny. Gallantry! what, from a fellow like you, a pitiful publican?

Tromf. Diable! publican? dat be good enough for de maker of pin.

Jenny. Here he comes.

Enter Dick Drugget.

Dick. Zounds, Mifs, here they all be!

Jenny.

Jenny. All! who?

Dick. Father, mother, and your aunt Clack, the milliner from out of Pall-Mall.—But, you feem flurried; there has nothing happened, I hope?

Jenny. Happened? that faucy Frenchman has taken fuch liberties!

Dicky. How!—Zounds, Sir, how dare you—

Tromf. Monfieur Dicky——

Jenny. Nay, the fellow is only fit to be laughed at: Befides, at prefent we want him.—Harkee, Monfieur, if you wifh to have your folly forgot, and not be expofed, as you richly deferve, you muft immediately lend your affiftance.

Tromf. Vid *plaifir.*

Jenny. Where can I conceal myfelf from my angry relations?

Tromf. Dere is but littel time for to tink. Ah-ha! I have it. I vill dis inftant put you into de *couvent,* vere my fifter is nun.

Jenny. But they will foon find me out, and force me from them.

Tromf. You muft pretend to have de grand inclination to become de bon catolick.

Jenny. And will that do?

Tromf. Never fear! Mademoifelle *eft bien riche*; and de French prieft never give up de convert ven fhe have got great deal of guinée, *jamais.*

Jenny.

Jenny. In the mean time, what is to become of my friend?

Tromf. De beſt way for Maiſter Dicky is to take de littel trip to Dunkirk or Boulogne, 'till matters be ſettle.

Jenny. May I venture, Monſieur, to truſt my-ſelf in your hands?

Tromf. By gar, Mademoiſelle, dere is more danger from your hand dan from mine!

Jenny. We Engliſh, Monſieur, are an odd ſort of people; it is near as dangerous to provoke our women as men.

Tromf. By gar, I believe ſo. No, no; *l'affair eſt faite;* I have done.—*Ma femme,* mylittel wife, ſhall conduct Mademoiſelle—LaJeuneſſe![*Calls.*

Enter La Jeuneſſe.

La Jeu. Monſieur?

Tromf. Go to my vife; tell her to take Ma-demoiſelle to de *couvent,* and leave her dere vid my ſiſter. After dinner, I vill bring you de news to de grate.

Jenny. Well, Dicky, adieu! expect to hear from me ſoon.

Dick. Be as quick as you will, I ſhall think it an age. Deareſt Jenny, farewell! [*Exit.*

Tromf. Juſque à revoir, Mademoiſelle!

Jenny. Servant, Monſieur Tromfort!

Tromf.

Tromf. Ma foi, Mademoiſelle be a great littel fool, to prefer Monſieur Dicky to ſuch anoder as me. By gar, de Englis voman have no judgment at all! ſhe vill repent by-and-by; more pity for ſhe!—La Jeuneſſe!

Enter La Jeuneſſe.

Have you ſent doſe bag of guinea to Dunkirk, to be melt?

La Jeu. Oui, Monſieur.

Tromf. Ver vell. [*Exit La Jeuneſſe.*]—*Apres tout* Meſſieurs *l'Anglois,* all de Englis people, be ver great fool, to come here, ſpend dere money, in ſearch after vat dey never will find! to ſhange dere roaſta beef and pudding, for our rotten ragout; ſee de comedy, de play, dey don't comprehend; talk vid de people dey don't underſtand; *tant mieux!* ſo much de better! In ver few year, I ſhut up my hotel, ſet up my coach, my caroſſe, and call myſelf monſieur le marquis de Guinea, in compliment to Meſſieurs *l'Anglois;* ver pritt title, by gar! ha, ha, ha! [*Exit.*

Enter La Jeuneſſe, Mr. and Mrs. Minnikin, Mrs. Clack, and Kit Codling.

Mrs. Min. This unnatural huſſy, to run thus

D   away

away from her parents! and into foreign parts, as they fay, amongft Pagans and Papifts, and a parcel of—And here we have been tofs'd and tumbled about, that I don't know whether I ftand upon my head or my heels.

Min. And then that lanthorn-jaw'd hound at the gate, to feize my tobacco-box! and I'll be fworn there was not a couple of pipe-fulls.

Mrs. Min. Ay, ay, poor toads, they are glad to get hold of any thing they can get. Well, if I once more fet fight of old Powl's, if ever they get me below Bridge again, unlefs a-pleafuring, perhaps, during the fummer, in a hoy to Margate—Pray, fon Codling, how long were we in failing over the fea?

Codl. I can tell you, madam Minnikin, exact to a minute; becaufe why, I have promis'd neighbour Index, the printer, to make obfer-wations on all the ftrange things that I fee, that he may print them next time, 'long with his Six Weeks Tour to the Continent. Let's fee; here is my Journal: [*reads*] " June the 10th, em-" barked at feven in the morning, at Dover, " aboard the Mercury, vind South and by Eaft; " nine o'clock, vind weer a little to the Veft; " fhell'd half a bufhel of peas; eleven o'clock, " vind ditto, eat ditto; twelve and half, pluck'd
" a couple

" a couple of fowls; very odd to fee how the
" vind blew the feathers about; *nota bene*, fea-
" thers will fwim in the falt fea."

Min. Vaft curus obfervations, indeed!

Mrs. Min. Nay, I always faid, fon Codling
had a good head of his own. Why, Matthew
Minnikin, if he goes on but as he begun, I don't
know but his'n may be as ufeful as many of the
Voyages that have been printed of late.

Min. Ay, Margery, if he could but get
fome ftrange beaftefles, or carry home a foreign
favage or two, for a fhow.

Mrs. Min. But go on, fon Codling, I beg!

Codl. " Two o'clock, road beginning to be
" confumedly rough, was fo much jolted, that
" I could not write any more."

Mrs. Min. Write? I'm fure I was not able
to ftand; fo they popp'd me into a hole in the
wall, I think they call'd it a *cabin*; Lord blefs
us, 'twas more liker a coffin!

Clack. The fea has been rather rumbuf-
tious, I own; but then, fifter, the land makes
us ample amends.

Mrs. Min. Amends! in what way?

Clack. Blefs me, fifter, how can you afk?
I profefs I feel myfelf quite a different perfon:
The people here are all fo gay, and well-
bred! Did not you obferve, when I accidentally

fneez'd,

fneez'd, how politely all the people pull'd off their hats?

Mrs. Min. Pfhaw! what fignifies their grins and grimaces, their fcrapes and congees? do you, fifter, ferioufly think, that the French folks are more cleverer than we?

Clack. Ridiculous! is there a mortal can doubt it? Why, without their affiftance, how fhould we be able to drefs ourfelves, or our victuals? And then, as to clevernefs, did you obferve thofe little children, as we came up from the key?

Mrs. Min. Yes; and to my thinking, I never faw fuch a parcel of brown brats in my life.

Clack. I declare I was afham'd, quite blufh'd for my country, to hear mere infants, quite babies, as I may fay, fputter French, more freer and glibber than your daughter Jane, who has had a French mafter thefe five years.

Mrs. Min. That's true, I muft own; but then I don't find that they be more cuter to get our lingo, than we to learn theirs.

Clack. Becaufe why, they think it beneath them.

Mrs. Min. Who the deuce be all thefe?

Enter feveral Porters with fmall parcels.

La Jeu. De porter from de cuftom-houfe, along vid your baggage.

Cod'l.

Codl. Baggage? zooks, any one of thefe might have carried it all.

Clack. Ay! there, there, brother, you have another proof of their breeding; all of them eager to be ufeful to ftrangers.

Min. Yes, pox take them, in hopes, I fuppofe, of being handfomely paid.—Well, Monfieurs, how much are you to have?

Clack. Fy, Mr. Minnikin! don't expofe your meannefs, the moment you are landed.—Monfieur, you will fatisfy thefe gentlemen for the trouble they have taken. And, Mr. Codling, do try and get us a good room, if you can.

La Jeu. Venez ici!

· [*Exeunt Porters, bowing and fcraping.*

Min. Hey-day! who the deuce have we here?

Mrs. Min. As I live, a couple of fhoe-blacks, with muffs and bag-wigs!

Enter Shoe-blacks, who bow with great ceremony, and take fnuff.

Min. There, there, Margery! doft thou fee? mark their fmirking, bowing and fneezing!

Clack. Ay, fifter Minnikin, there! you fee how courteous and civil the very loweft people are here: Shew me a fhopkeeper, in

your

your whole ward, that can do his honours fo
well! See how politely they offer their fnuff
to each other; and look! if the fweet little
creatures are not fet down to cards on their
ftools!

Min. Yes, yes; I fee well enough.

Clack. Not like our vulgar fellows, at Putt
or All-fours, but a party at Piquet, I'll be
fworn!

*Enter La Jeuneffe, Luke Lapelle, and Gregory
Gingham.*

La Jeu. Dis vay, my lor! one, two, dree ftep;
take care-a, my lor!

Mrs. Min. Blefs me, my dear, if here a'n't
Mr. Lappelle, from Bond-Street! and neigh-
bour Gingham, as fure as a gun! frefh from
Paris, I warrant.

Min. Well met, neighbour Gingham! What,
you've been fetching home fafhions, I reckon?

Ging. Hufh, Mafter Minnikin! there is no
need to make proclamation in foreign parts, of
what bufinefs we be.

Clack. Brother Minnikin's tongue will now-
and-then run too faft for his wit.

Min. Nay, I faid nothing, I am fure.

Lap. Excufé moi, Monfieur Minnikin! you
mentioned

mentioned fetching of fashions; and that, as the French say, was *tantaramount* to calling us tailors.

Clack. The very same thing.

Min. Why, sure, Gregory Gingham, thee be'st not ashamed of thy calling, be'st?

Ging. That is another man's matter, you knows: How is it our fault, (d'ye mind me?) if the French folks will take us for lords? They saw something in us that was above the vulgar, I reckon.

Mrs. Min. Nay, for the matter of that, Matthew, it is at worst but being quit with Mounseer; for, I'll be sworn, there are many of their Counts and Marquisses that comes over to us, (aye, and are received by the best quality too, at their tables) who, if the truth was known, are little better than tailors at home.

Codl. Right! well said, Madam Minnikin! With this odds in their favour, (plague take 'em!) that them there fellows make a good hand and profit by their pride and presumption; whilst our foolish folks are forced to pay pretty high fees for their titles. I reckon, your *lordships* were swingingly sous'd on the road?

Ging. To say truth, the bills did mount pretty
high,

high, and we did not chufe to chaffer with them, becaufe why, we wa'n't willing to bring a dif-grace on our dignity.

Clack. Wifely done, for the honour of England !

Codl. Honour? I can't fay that ever I heard that Old England received much honour from tailors; unlefs, indeed, when they lifted in Elliot's Light-horfe.

Lap. That may be the cafe, Mafter Minnikin, with thofe of the trade who live in the city; but I would have you to know, the knights of the needle are another fort of people at our end of the town.

Clack. Doubtlefs.

Lap. It is not in the fafhions only that we take the lead; we rule likewife over the *Belles Lettres*, as the French call them.

Min. How?

Lap. Give laws to the drama; damn a play when we pleafe; or hifs an actor off the ftage, when we take a diflike to the rafcal.

Codl. Ay? it is the firft I ever heard of a tailor's goofe hiffing !

Lap. Yes, yes; why, I myfelf, at the head of my journeymen, have more than once played the part of THE PUBLICK.

Min. You furprize me !

Lap.

Lap. And am known, at all our houses of call, by the name of *Tom Town.*

Clack. Mr. Lapelle, you are but losing your labour: Honest good sort of people enough; but mere cits, quite ignorant of what is going on in the world !

Lap. Yes, yes, they look of that cut; not of the right stuff, as the French say, to make *bucks desprits* on.

Clack. And pray what news is stirring in Paris ?

Lap. Tojours gay, as the French say, Mrs. Clack.

Mrs. Min. I reckon there be powers of our country folks there.

Lap. I suppose so; for I saw a good many aukward people, as they say, *à la comedy*, and at the *Colossus*; but I chose to avoid them.

Mrs. Min. And why so ?

Codl. I reckon there were some of his masters amongst them; and it would not have been decent to be too forward, for a tradesman, like he.

Lap. Pardonnez moi! that was not it ; it is always the rule with me, when I travels, to avoid *les Anglois,* as the French say, the English, as much as I can.

Codl. I reckon the French, as they don't know his trade, are more politer and civil.

Lap. No; there's a roughness, a *bourgoisy,*

E   about

about our barbarians, that is not at all to my tafte; not a bit, as the French fay, to my *gout*.

Clack. I don't wonder at it. I hope you left the royal family all in good health.

Lap. Yes; Mr. *le Roi*, as the French fay, looked pretty jolly; and I was at his grand *couvert*, and *cowfhee* a-Sunday: His majefty looked at me very hard.

Clack. Indeed?

Mrs. Min. Ay; wondering, I fuppofe, how fuch a one as he could contrive to get in.

Lap. This relation of yours, Mrs. Clack, is but a low kind of a body.—No, no, Mrs. Minnikin; his majefty and I have been acquainted, many a time and oft have I been at court, when he was only the *dolphin*.

Clack. Pray, how long, Mr. Lapelle, was you coming from Paris?

Lap. Two days and a night.

Clack. Are the accommodations good upon the road?

Lap. Their horfes, their *chevauxes*, as the French call them, are not quite fo nimble as our'n; but then, to make amends, like the French, I *courier* the poft, without ftopping; unlefs, perhaps, to take a flight *repas* of a bit of *jambun*, or a *hamlet*.

Min. But how do you like your jaunt,

neighbour

neighbour Gingham? You are rather silent, I think.

Lap. This, you know, is only Gingham's first trip: Besides, to like Paris, a man must *parle vous* in perfection; speak their lingor perfectly well.

Ging. For the matter of that, master Lapelle, the postilions did not seem to take very readily all that you said on the road.

Lap. Them there fellows! how should they? mere country bumpkins! little better, as we say in French, than a parcel of *pheasants!*

Clack. Ay, hogs, I suppose, like our own.

Lap. True, Mrs. Clack; quite *cowchans*, as we say.

Mrs. Min. Have they pretty good victuals in these parts, neighbour Gingham?

Ging. Victuals? soup, that tasted as if wrung from a dish-clout, and rags stewed in vinegar, are all the victuals I have seen.

Lap. Ah! poor Gingham has a true English stomach; nothing will do but substantials; he has no taste for *ragoutes, intermeats,* and *rottis.*

Ging. Nay, you know, at the last town, my wife fished out a large piece of blue apron, upon the top of her fork.

Mrs. Min. What! did Mrs. Gingham come with you?

Ging.

Ging. Yes; and is about as well pleafed as myfelf.

Mrs. Min. Where is fhe?

Ging. In a room hard-by, with Mrs. Lapelle.

Lap. How often have I cautioned you not to give her that name here in France? fuppofe any of the people fhould hear you!

Clack. What, then, I fuppofe it is not Mrs. Lapelle, that is, your real wife, that is with you?

Lap. Yes, yes; but you know nothing can be fo vulgar in France, as voyaging about with one's wife; fo I make her pafs for my miftrefs, and always calls her *Mademoifelle.*

Clack. And fhe fares never the worfe, I'll be fworn.

Lap. *Au contraire,* as they fay; befides, it is the onlieft method to keep her to one's felf.

Mrs. Min. How fo?

Lap. No Frenchman fcruples to make love to a wife; becaufe why, 'tis not the fafhion for the hufband to care a farthing about her; but to fe-duce a man's miftrefs, that he is imagined to love, is a crime that is never forgiven.

Clack. Lord, Mr. Lapelle, we are like the French in a great many things.

Lap. Yes, we endeavour; and, to fay truth, improve every day in our morals.

Clack. But mayn't we join the ladies within?

Lap.

Lap. By all means—but mind the caution I gave!—Yes; Mademoifelle and I by accident picked up Gingham and wife. We met them in the *Fauxbourg* of *St. German*; and as we were to fet out about the fame time, we thought it would be, as the French fay, for us four to come to Calais together, an agreeable *tête-à-tête* on the road.

Clack. Well, I fhould like vaftly to fee Paris before my return; but the journey is fo very expenfive! coft a world of money, no doubt?

Lap. Why, as I know how to manage, not altogether fo much: It is true, we paid our bills like lords, on the road; but it fhall go hard, Mrs. Clack, if I don't make the real lords re-fund, when I fend in their bills.

Clack. All the reafon in life.

Lap. This, with a good cargo of lace con-veyed by Mademoifelle, and fome rich fuits that I know how to fmuggle fafely to Dover, will, I fhould think, carry me fcot-free to Bond-Street. —But, pray, what brings all your family?

Clack. We will inform you within.

Lap. Gingham, you will efcort Mrs. Minni-kin? Mrs. Clack, as the French fay, will you accept of my *brafs*?   [*Exeunt, with ceremony.*

A C T

A C T II.

A French Apartment.

Enter Mr. and Mrs. Minnikin and Mrs. Clack.

Mrs. Minnikin.

I TELL you, Matthew, it is all a purtence, merely to keep out of our hands ! Why, what fhould fhe do in a convent ?

Min. Mayhap, Margery, fhe may take it in her head to turn nun.

Mrs. Min. Lord, Matthew, how can'ft think of any fuch a thing ? She nun ! no, no ; fhe's more likely by half to bring people into the world, than to take any one out on't. What fay you, fifter Clack ?

Clack. I am pretty much of your mind, I muft confefs ; but we fhall know more of the matter when Kit Codling comes back.

Min. D'ye think they'll permit'n to fee her ?

Mrs. Min. That, I fuppofe, will depend on herfelf. Oh, here comes Mr. Codling.

Enter Codling.

Well, fon, what news from the runagate ? have you feen her ?

Codl.

Codl. Not I : They firſt ſhew'd me up to a room with iron rails at one end, like a begging-grate; and upon ringing the bell, there popped out of t'other ſide the bars an old gentlewoman, dreſt in a blanket, with a black handkerchief over her head.

Mrs. Min. Yes; I have heard the Papiſhes have ſuch dreſſes amongſt them : Who was ſhe ?

Codl. I took her to be one of the clargywo- men that belong to the place. I aſked, if they had veigled one Miſs Minnikin into their clutches, in hopes to make her a Papiſh : At the word *veigled,* the old woman turn'd up the whites of her eyes, and with her hands croſs her ſto- mach, like a child that is ſaying her catechiſe, made a jaculation; I fancy, in the outlandiſh tongue; upon which, I told her to let me have none on her hypocriſy canting, but to anſwer direct to my queſtions.

Clack. How rude ! it was lucky ſhe did not underſtand you.

Codl. Underſtand me ? yes, as well as you do : Pho, mun, they be all Engliſhwomen that be locked up in that church. She owned that Miſs Jenny was there.

Mrs. Min. She did ?

Codl. Then I aſked if I could not change a few words with her, by way of a little diſcourſe; they

they faid no, becaufe why, Mifs was out of order at prefent.

Min. A pretence; nothing elfe.

Codl. So I reckon. Then I defired the gentlewoman to open the hatch, and let me in doors to fee her, for I had a word or two for her private ear from her parents; upon that, the old goffop fet up fuch a grumbling, called me profligate harrytick, and wondered I could be fo empiety to think they ever fuffered a man to enter their doors; 'pon that, I told her, that if none of her complifhes were more handfome than fhe, ecod they might open their doors without any great danger; ha, ha! this made the old one as mad as the deuce!

Clack. I tould you what would happen, if you fent fuch a rough creature as he.

Codl. No; we grew more milder at laft; and fhe offer'd to fhew her, if her father and mother would come.

Mrs. Min. Then, Matthew, let us go to her this inftant! Son Codling will fhew us the way.

Codl. For the matter of that, I don't believe you will fpeed much better than me.

Clack. And why not?

Codl. When I afk'd her, if as how fhe thought Jenny had ferufly a mind to turn to their way, fhe faid fhe didn't make the leaft doubt on't;

for

for that Mifs had all the true outward and vifible figns of an inward vacation.

Mrs. Min. Who have we here?

Enter Father O'Donnovan, a Capuchin.

Codl. I don't know; a mountebank; I reckon; or mayhap a man that fhews fleight of hand.

O'Don. Save you, good jontlemen!

Mrs. Min. No, no; it is an Englifhman, I know by his tongue.—Well, friend, who and what are you?

O'Don. Plaife you, I am a poor Capuchin, that belongs to this convent here in the town.

Codl. Capuchin? and pray, honeft friend, what trade is that in the French?

O'Don. Trade! the devil a bit of a trade that it is: By my fhoul, if I had a mind to be of a trade, do you think I would have quitted my haymaking in England?

Mrs. Min. What is it, then, that you follow?

O'Don. It is a kind of profeffion, my dear.

Mrs. Min. A profeffion!

O'Don. Ay; we makes profeffions of poverty, that we may be fure to want for nothing as long as we live.

Codl. And how do you get what you want?

O'Don. By afking it from thofe that can give it.

F   *Codl.*

Codl. Godfo! then you are a beggar, I fancy.

O'Don. Who? a beggar? what the divil put that in your head?

Mrs. Min. What d'ye call yourfelf elfe?

O'Don. I am only a mendicant, honey.

Codl. I wonders you prefer fo idle a life.

O'Don. And why fo? d'ye think that I would not rather that other people fhould work for me, than work for myfelf? not that I fhould mind working neither, but only becaafe it is fo very laborious.

Mrs. Min. And are folks now very charitable in this here part of the world?

O'Don. Charitable! the devil of any charity's in it: It is, honey, a Chriftian kind of a bargain, ftruck up among us, I think.

Claik. A bargain?

O'Don. Ay; whilft they work for us, we pray for them; they take care of our bodies, and, in return, my dear, we take care of their fhouls.

Codl. Souls! never ftir, father, if this ben't one of their friars!

Mrs. Min. Sure as can be, fon Codling has hit it. Who can tell, hufband, as he is our countryman, and one of the gang, but, for a little fpill of money, he may put us in a way to get our daughter out of their clutches?

M n.

Min. It is but trying, however.

Mrs. Min. And pray, good Sir, by what name may we call you?

O'Don. Father O'Donnovan, at your humble farvice.

Mrs. Min. Will you do us the favour to ftep a little this way?—Son Codling, have a look-out, that we ben't interrupted.—Why, you muft know, that a daughter of ours has run away from her friends, and *voluns, noluns,* taken fhelter here in a cloifter.

O'Don. Run away from her friends? By my fhoul, that was very foolifhly done!

Mrs. Min. Now if you could put us in a way, by hook or by crook, to get her out of the convent——

O'Don. Me? what, me? to get a parfon out of a convent?

Mrs. Min. If you would be fo kind to affift——

O'Don. Fy! confider, woman, what you are afking.

Min. Nay, Sir!

O'Don. Upon my confcience, here is one of the moft blackeft confpiracies broke out againft Popery, fince gunpowder-treafon.

Mrs. Min. Patience, fweet Sir!

O'Don. To tempt one of my order to be guilty of facredncfs!

Mrs.

Mrs. Min. Indeed, good Sir, I had no such thing in my head.

O'Don. Pace, woman! What is it better than sacrednefs, to break into a convent, and take any cratur out by compulfion?

Mrs. Min. But, Sir——

O'Don. I tell you, even to force a young woman from thence, that is willing to lave it, is one of the biggeft robberies that can be committed.

Mrs. Min. My dear——

O'Don. And, to extenuate the matter, here is a dutiful poor young body, that flies from her parents, and takes refuge in the arms of the church——

Mrs. Min. Hear me a word, reverend Sir!

O'Don. We fhall fee what the Commandant will fay to this bufinefs! Take my word for it, my friends, you will be all faaz'd in an inftant, and locked up in prifon aboard the gallies for the reft of your lives.

Mrs. Min. Mercy on us!—Sifter Clack, try if you can't mollify his choler a little, or we fhall be clap'd up in the quifition directly.

Clack. Can you, reverend Sir, be fo cruel to your country-folks here——

O'Don. Pace, woman!

Clack. Indeed they had no bad intentions; they only wanted to afk your reverence's

advice,

advice, and meant to leave a fmall fum in your
.hands——

O'Don. Sum? do you main to infult me?
Don't you know, woman, that we muft never
touch money?

Clack. To beftow upon poor objects that
want it; but, if fo be your reverence is for-
bidden to touch it, why, to be fure, we won't
dare to——

O'Don. Why, lookee, miftrefs; to handle
money is againft the rules of our order, which
we dare not break through: If, indeed, it was
put into a purfe, why, there would be no occafion, d'ye fee, for me to touch it.

Clack. Brother Minnikin, have you ever a
purfe?

Mrs. Min. Here, here is mine, fifter Clack.

O'Don. Why, as you faam to be well-dif-
pofed people, and only want a little wholefome
advice; why, that, d'ye fee, may alter the cafe.

Mrs. Min. Nothing elfe, indeed, reverend
Sir.

O'Don. Why, d'ye mind me, it would not
be dacent for me to ftir in this matter; becaafe why, as we are monks, you know, it is
our duty to bring over and pervert as many fhouls
as we can.

Mrs. Min. True, reverend Sir; but there is
nothing

nothing of that in the matter; the girl, Heaven knows, has no more mind to be preverted than any of us.

O'Don. How! more fhame for her! but may I belave you?

Mrs. Min. All a pretence, nothing elfe; fhe is run away with an idle 'prentice of ours, to avoid that young man there before you.

O'Don. Have you brought with you no letters of recommendation to any ftrangers of your acquaintance, that live in this town?

Mrs. Min. We know no mortal; we have not been landed an hour.

O'Don. Becaafe a little intereft in this cafe would go a great way; not but there are fome of our own country folks, that live here in great credit: Perhaps you may have known them at home.

Mrs. Min. Does your reverence remember their names?

O'Don. There is Mr. Mac-Rappum, that lives in the Square, one of the beft-natured craturs alive: He got the jail-diftemper, by attending his own trial at the Old-Bailey.

Mrs. Min. Poor gentleman!

O'Don. So the judge advifed him to try for feven years the air of America.

Mrs. Min. And did he reap any benefit?

O'Don.

O'Don. He has put off the jaunt for awhile.

Mrs. Min. Why fo?

O'Don. I don't know; they talk that that place is all in combuftion at prefent; fo being a paceable man, he chofe to be fet down here in his way.

Mrs. Min. Doft know him, Matthew?

Min. Not I.

O'Don. Then there is one 'Squire Copywell, that is but lately come over; a very fafatious, humourfome man: He laid a bet with a frind of his, out of fun, that he would draw a bill in the hand-writing of Sir Timothy Tradewell, fo like that the banker fhould pay it without hefitation.

Mrs. Min. And did he?

O'Don. You may fay that: But, when they come to find out the miftake, the banker, being a crufty dull fellow, and not underftand-ing a joke, talked of going to law with the 'fquire.

Mrs. Min. Lord blefs us! how could they—

O'Don. Nay, I don't know, my fhoul; them there Englifh have fome ftrange maxims amongft them; fo the 'fquire, not caring to throw away his money to lawyers, chofe to come and live here, rather than make any more words of the matter.

Clack.

Clack. I'd have done the very fame thing, had I been the 'fquire.

O'Don. Nay, for the matter of that, you have no more manners than morality among you in England.

Mrs. Min. How, reverend Sir! I thought we was remarkable for——

O'Don. Pace, woman, and hold your pallaver! Was there ever fuch ill breeding as Lord Con-ftant's to Sir Henry Hornbeam, that lives hard-by here at Ardres.

Clack. Indeed, I never heard nothing about it.

O'Don. My lord was obligated to go about his affairs into the North for a month, and left his difconfolate lady behind him in London.

Mrs. Min. Poor gentlewoman!

O'Don. Upon which, his friend Sir Henry ufed to go and ftay there all the day, to amufe and divert her.

Mrs. Min. How good-natured that was in Sir Henry!

O'Don. Nay, he carried his friendfhip much further than that; for my lady, as there was many highwaymen and footpads about, was afraid that fome of them would break into the houfe, and fo defired Sir Henry to lie there every night.

Mrs. Min. Good foul! and he did, I dare fay?

O'Don.

O'Don. To be fure: There is not a more politer man in the world. So, hearing in the middle of the night a little noife below ftairs, he run'd down to fee what was the matter; finding all fafe, in coming up again, he chanced to make a little miftake.

Mrs. Min. How fo?

O'Don. Inftead of going to his own bed, he ftepped into my lady's.

Clack. That might happen very well, in the dark.

O'Don. And there falling afleep, never once found out his miftake 'till the maid came up in the morning.

Clack. He muft have been vaftly furprized, to be fure.

Mrs. Min. And, I warrant me, fo was my lady.

O'Don. Without doubt. But now comes the upfhot of all: I reckon, you fuppofe my lord thought himfelf much obliged to Sir Henry?

Clack. To be fure.

O'Don. Not he, by my fhoul! nay, more worfer than that, he had the ill manners to bring an action againft him.

Clack. What, after Sir Harry had told him the ftory?

O'Don. Ay, and my lady likewife; fo it muft be

G   true,

true, as you know, becaafe why, they could not both be miftaken.

Clack. There was no danger of that.

O'Don. So, Sir Harry, not chufing to live any longer amongft fuch under-bred people, has fettled here for his life.

Clack. Why, as there is fo much good company, it muft be vaft agreeable living here, I fhould think.

O'Don. You may fay that; and indeed this place is fo pleafant, that every day one ingenus parfon or other comes over to live. Upon my fhoul, among ourfelves, I belave the folks on your fide the water begin to grow a little jealous.

Clack. No wonder.

O'Don. Infomuch, that they have made application to the magiftrates here to fend fome of them forcibly back.

Mrs. Min. But I dare fay the French were more politer than that.

O'Don. To be fure. Indeed, out of compaffion, they have compelled three or four that were poor to return; becaafe why, it coudn't be very agreeable to them, you know, to live here without money.

Mrs. Min. To be fure.

O'Don.

O'Don. And then, the Englifh are indulged in the free exercife of their religion.

Mrs. Min. Oh, then they go to church?

O'Don. No, no; if they find 'em preaching or praying, they hang up the minifter, and fend the congregation all to the gallies.

Mrs. Min. Doft hear that, Matthew Min-nikin?

O'Don. So now, as I was a-telling, if you can get any frind to fpeak to the——Boo-boo-boo! upon my fhoul, I had like to have forgot the moft materialift parfon of all: Does any of you know Lady Kitty Crocodile?

Clack. Lady Kitty! nobody better; I have had the honour of working for her ladyfhip this many years.

O'Don. Then your bufinefs will be done in a trice. Between ourfelves, the ladies always rule the roaft in this part of the world.

Clack. I dare believe her ladyfhip will be very willing to ferve us.

O'Don. I don't doubt it at all; fhe is one of the moft worthieft women alive: She coudn't bear to ftay in England after the death of her hufband, every thing there put her fo much in mind of her lofs. Why, if fhe met by accident with one of his boots, it always fet her a-crying; indeed, the poor gentlewoman was a perfect Niobe.

Clack.

Clack. Indeed, I found her ladyſhip in a very incontionable way, when I waited on her upon the mournful occaſion. Indeed, ſhe was rather more chearful when ſhe tried on her weeds; and no wonder, for it is a dreſs vaſtly becom-. ing, eſpecially to people inclined to be fat. But I was in hopes, by this timé ſhe had got over her griefs.

O'Don. Not at all, indeed. Indeed, with the French ſhe is faſatious and pleaſant enough; but ſhe no ſooner ſets ſight on any thing Engliſh, than the tears burſt out like a whirl-wind.

Clack. Then, if we can do without it, we won't trouble her ladyſhip.

Mrs. Min. True; we will firſt try, ſiſter, what we can do at the convent.

O'Don. By all means: And, d'ye hear, you need not mention any thing about the purſe; you underſtand me ?

Clack. Oh, father, you need not fear us.

O'Don. Nay, it is not for that; but becaaſe one's charity, you know, ſhould be private; and therefore, to devulge it would take away moſt of the merit.   [*Exit.*

Clack. True, true. What's next to be done ?

Mrs. Min. Why, we had beſt go after the wench to the convent.

                                  Clack.

Clack. But take care what you fay! you fee what a hobble we had like to have got into.

Mrs. Min. Never you fear; I warrant, I knows how to behave myfelf.   ·   [*Exeunt.*

Scene, a Convent.

Enter Abbefs and Jenny.

Abbefs. Only, daughter, confider to what temptation you are expofed in the world.

Jenny. The more merit, mother, then in me, to refift them.

Abbefs. Attacked by enemies from every· quarter.

Jenny. I am a girl of fpirit, mother, and am determined to face them.

Abbefs. But they will be too powerful, child, for you to refift.

Jenny. Then, like abler officers, I muft fur-render. I fuppofe there will be no danger of their refufing me quarter.

Abbefs. Daughter, daughter, I am afraid your affeftions are carnal.

Jenny. Mother, mother, they are like other girls of my age.

Abbefs. Why won't you accept a fpiritual fpoufe?

Jenny.

Jenny. Becaufe I have found one of flefh and blood much more to my mind.

Abbefs. Confider, that is a union that will continue for ever.

Jenny. And do you call that a recommendation, good mother?

Abbefs. The other, child, muft be finally diffolved by death.

Jenny. Like many of my countrywomen, perhaps, I mayn't have patience to tarry altogether fo long. But come, mother, I can, I believe, give good guefs at your meaning: You have a notion that I fhould bring a pretty good fortune to this fpoufe of your recommendation?

Abbefs. True, daughter.

Jenny. To which, as I never heard of any children produced by this unaccountable union, you will fucceed? Now I muft tell you, I ha'n't a farthing of fortune.

Abbefs. Daughter?

Jenny. I am entirely dependant upon father, who, I am pofitively fure, won't part with a farthing to you. He give any thing to your church, as you call it? why, he's never fo happy as when he can rob our own vicar at home of his dues.

Abbefs. What, daughter, have you no feparate portion?

Jenny.

Jenny. Not a doit.

Abbefs. And your father fo fixed an heretic as you have defcribed him?

Jenny. Hates a Papifh worfer than poifon.

Abbefs. Well, child, as I find you have no immediate call to the veil, I fhall at this time prefs it no further: Your beft way will, I think, be to return to your father.

Jenny. Not quite fo foon, if you pleafe. I have told you what induced me to leave him; now, if you will fcreen me from his purfuit, 'till I can otherwife difpofe of myfelf, tho' I am not rich, I have a few guineas here that will thank you.

Abbefs. Why, as the compelling a daughter to marry is a profanation of one of our facraments, I am bound in duty, if I can, to prevent it.

Jenny. Is it? gad, I like that part of your creed well enough.

Enter a Nun.

Nun. The father and mother of that amiable child are now at the grate.

Jenny. Lord, good mother, what fhall I do?

Abbefs. Let them know, fhe fhall attend them directly.   [*Exit Nun.*

Jenny. How, mother!

Abbefs.

Abbefs. Fear nothing! if they infift on the taking you hence, urge an affection you feel for our faith, and that you wifh to wait here for our ghoftly inftructions; in fuch a cafe, this is a fecure fanctuary from the fecular arm.

Jenny. I underftand you, good mother. [*Exe.*

Scene, the Grate.

Enter Mr. and Mrs. Minnikin, Mrs. Clack, and Codling.

Min. This jade is the plague of our lives!

Mrs. Min. Peace, Matthew! by rough means we fhall gain nothing, I am fure ; let us try what a little mollification will do. Son Codling, keep out of fight, if you pleafe.

Enter the Abbefs and Jenny.

Abbefs. This, I prefume, is the perfon you want.

Mrs. Min. Yes, Miftrefs, this is the party, indeed.—So, Jenny, how could you be fo naughty, child, to run away from your father and me ?

Min. Yes, and to confort with a parcel of Pap——

Mrs. Min. Peace, Matthew! there be good and bad of all forts, as they fay.

Min.

Min. True; and I warrant her she'll make choice of the worst.

Mrs. Min. Well, but, come, Matthew, it is never too late to repent.

Clack. True, sister; and I dare say, my niece is ready to return back with us, and will do every thing we can desire her.

Jenny. I am sensible of the respect and duty I owe to my parents——

Mrs. Min. Very well said, child! it is a long lane that has no turning.

Jenny. And shall always be ready to obey their commands.

Min. Do you hear, Mistress? then open the doors, and let her come out.

Jenny. Pardon me, Sir; that cannot be.

Min. Why not?

Jenny. Because a much more important duty detains me.

Min. And pray what pretty duty may that be?

Jenny. This pious and reverend lady will tell you.

Min. Come, mistress, let us have it then.

Abbess. Your daughter, son, by a miraculous operation, has had her eyes opened to the perilous paths in which she was straying.

Min. Yes, yes, she has wandered long enough, to be sure.

H   *Abbess.*

Abbefs. And has begged our advice to direct her in the right road.

Min. And if fhe takes it, it will be the firft time in her life.

Abbefs. Say not fo, fon; you are too rafh in your judgment.

Min. To come to the proof, will fhe marry the young man we have provided?

Abbefs. She has provided a better match for herfelf.

Min. The devil fhe has! what, a 'prentice-boy that wants two years to be out of his time?

Abbefs. Son, I don't comprehend you.

Min. Dick Drugget, I mean; as arrant a fcape-grace——

Abbefs. Son, I know no fuch perfon as Drugget.

Min. What, he has chang'd his name, I fup-pofe, fince he came over! like enough.

Abbefs. Son, we err, I believe, as to the perfon; the fpoufe your daughter wifhes to wed, is Saint Francis.

Min. Saint Francis! who the devil is he? what, has fhe pick'd up a Frenchman already? like enough: But if that be the cafe, Miftrefs, you may give my fervice to Mr. Saint Francis, and tell him he fhall never touch a fingle penny of mine as long as he lives.

Abbefs.

Abbefs. Saint Francis ſtands in need of no fortune.

Min. He is ſo rich? ſo much the better for he. And you may over and above tell him, notwithſtanding ſhe looks ſo demure, that he could not have met with ſuch a headſtrong, ob-ſtinate, peremptory vixen, if he had ſearched all the country round.

Abbefs. Saint Francis will, notwithſtanding, cheriſh the dear child in his boſom.

Min. Will he? then, if the dear child don't kick his guts out in leſs than a month, ſhe is confoundedly altered! But come, Miſtreſs; mayhap, we may find friends here, although we be ſtrangers: We'll ſee if there be no laws againſt kidnapping other folks' children away!

Abbefs. You grow indecent, ſon; we muſt leave you.

Min. In England now I would have horpus'd-corpus'd her out of your hands in an hour!

Abbefs. Daughter, pay your reverence to your relations! *[Jenny curtſies, and retires from the grate, with the Abbefs.*

Min. An hypocritical ſlut! And harkee, Miſtreſs! before I goes, I will tell you a bit of my mind: Notwithſtanding your whining and canting, and ſanctified looks, I don't think you are a bit better than you ſhould be, d'ye

ſee

fee me; and, if the truth was known, you are little better, I believe, than an old matchmaking bawd!

Mrs. Min. Matthew, confider where you are! have a care what you fay!

Min. Prithee, woman, be quiet! Lofers have leave to fpeak in all countries, I hope.

Mrs. Min. And of what ufe is your fpeaking?

Clack. True, fifter. But come; let us go to Lady Kitty, as the friar advifed us; perhaps fhe may put us in a way.

Mrs. Min. Right, fifter. Come, Matthew, there is no time to be loft.

Min. Loft? we had better leave her to her own wicked ways: She will find that punifhment enough, in the end.

Mrs. Min. But fhe is our daughter, Matthew, you know; let us do our duty, however.

Min. Well, well! Come, fon Codling!

Codl. I'll follow you, father, when I have made an obfervation or two, to put into neighbour Index's Tower.—" The clargywomen in thefe " parts don't ufe any linen; and inftead of doing " like our'n, they wear their woollen fmocks " over the reft of their cloaths. *Nota bene*, if " they can catch any young women into their " clutches, they locks them up in dens like wild " beaftefes, that are kept in the Tower." [*Exe.*

Scene,

Scene, a Hotel.

Enter Miss Lydell and Hetty.

Miss L. Sure never was so capricious a being!

Hetty. Not of the same mind two minutes together! I am aftonifhed, Mifs, how you are able to bear it.

Miss L. I only wait for a fair occasion to quit her ladyfhip; fuch a one, I mean, as would juftify me to my friends.

Hetty. For that, Mifs, you can't be long at a lofs.

Miss L. Ah, Hetty, it is impoffible for you to guefs at the half of her art : My relations, feduced by her frequent profeffions, trufted me to her care, expecting, what I am fatisfied never will happen, a permanent eftablifhment for me by means of her favour.

Hetty. Why, fure, Mifs, fhe can't for fhame but do fomething handfome for you, after having drag'd you in her train, as I may fay, almoft over the world.

Miss L. There, Hetty, is the fource of her prefent behaviour : She knows what fhe has promifed, and wants to force me to fome indif-

creet

creet act of impatience, as an apology for the
breach of her faith.

Hetty. Ay? is she so cunning as that?

Miss L. For at the same time that she is
teazing, torturing, and loading me with every
mortification in private, you see with what particular regard and attention she affects to treat
me in public.

Hetty. True enough, I must own, Miss; exactly like her pretended grief for Sir John: She
howls and cries over the poor boot, for all the
world like the strange creature I have read of.

Miss L. Hush, Hetty! she is here.

Enter Lady Kitty Crocodile.

L. Kitty. In close committee, I see! What
mischief are you two brewing together?—I am
astonish'd, Miss Lydell, at your seducing my
servants; is this a proper return, Miss, for all
the obligations you owe me?

Miss L. I am sorry your ladyship should
think me capable——

L. Kitty. Capable?—Leave the room, with
your inquisitive impertinent face! You want
some tale to run tattling with, to the rest of
the crew. [*To Hetty.*

Hetty. Crew? I don't understand what your
ladyship means by the *crew*; tho' we are servants,

vants, we may be as good Chriſtians as other people, I hope; and tho', to be ſure——

L. Kitty. Hold your inſolent tongue, and quit the room, when I bid you!

Hetty. Crew?—With all my heart; I have no objeſtion to quitting the room, nor the houſe neither, for the matter of that. *Crew,* indeed; marry come up! [*Exit.*

L. Kitty. So, Miſs! theſe are the fruits of your little hypocritical plots; theſe leſſons have been taught them by you.

Miſs L. Me, Madam? Can your ladyſhip ſuppoſe, that I would deſcend ſo low as to——

L. Kitty. Deſcend, Miſs? I.don't underſtand you: Pray, in what reſpeſt are you ſo much better than they? Is it becauſe I have permitted you to ſit at my table, that you give yourſelf theſe airs of importance? Though your father was parſon of the pariſh, yet I hope I was not obliged at his death to provide for all his beggarly tribe.

Miſs L. Madam, I never preſumed——

L. Kitty. And yet, has not my generoſity been extended to every branch? There was your mother; did not I, by my own ſingle intereſt, get her into the Alms-Houſe at Bromley; where, except meat, drink, and cloaths, ſhe is amply provided with every thing a woman of her condition can want?

Miſs L.

Miss L. `I never denied——

L. Kitty. Was not your brother Tom, Miss, made a guinea-pig upon my recommendation?

,Miss L. Granted, Madam.

L. Kitty. And as to you, did not I, for no reason that I know, unless indeed that you are a distant relation, take you into my house, put you above my own woman, and make you one of my maids of honour at once?

Miss L. I hope, Madam, I have not proved ungrateful.

L. Kitty. No, Miss? How often have I caught you ogling and throwing out lures to Sir John in his life-time?

Miss L. I hope, Madam, Sir John never charged me with any designs of that nature.

L. Kitty. No; there was your security, Miss; you knew he was too generous and good to expose your infamous arts; but you could not conceal them from me!

Miss L. Nay, for Heaven's sake, Madam—

L. Kitty. In Italy too, there was Prince Pincoffi and Cardinal Grimsky; you could not help throwing out your traps to ensnare them.

Miss L. Me, Madam?

L. Kitty. Yes, you; what else, at my assemblies, could make them prefer your conversation to mine? I hope you have not the impudence

dence to fuppofe, that your perfon and figure would bear any comparifon.

Mifs L. Madam, I never prefumed——

L.. Kitty. Befides, Mifs, you know I never durft carry you with me to any conference I had with the Pope, for fear you fhould be trying fome of your coquetifh airs upon him.

Mifs L. Mercy upon me!

L. Kitty. And here too, Colonel Crofby, the only decent man in the town, when I was in Calais before, never miffed my toilet a morning; but now, when he comes, won't tarry a moment, unlefs indeed when you are in waiting.

Mifs L. I am fo confufed at the ftrange charges your ladyfhip brings, that I proteft I don't know what anfwer to make!

L. Kitty. I do really believe you. But you fee, Mifs, all your little contrivances are fully difcovered; and I fhould tell you, Mifs Lydell, that you are the moft artificial, cunning, hypocritical, mifchievous minx, that ever I met with, but my humanity and my good breeding prevents me: A woman of quality fhould never lofe fight of her ftation.

Mifs L. Was I capable of but half the crimes your ladyfhip lays to my charge, I fhould deteft myfelf full as much as your ladyfhip hates me. But I can't wifh, Madam, that your ladyfhip

I   fhould

should keep about your perfon a young creature to whom you have been pleafed to take fuch an averfion: Send me, therefore, Madam, to my poor mother; her age and infirmities muft want my affiftance.

L. Kitty. Who hinders you, Mifs? You may go when you pleafe.

Mifs L. Your ladyfhip will fend with me fome perfon of confidence? or, at leaft, a line to my mother, intimating, that I have neither difhonoured myfelf, or deferted your ladyfhip?

L. Kitty. So! here is another ftroke of your art! You want to perfuade people, that, through caprice, grown tired of your company, I have the cruelty to throw you at once upon the wide world: No, Mifs! that won't do; you fhould be a little more careful to cover the hook.

Enter a Servant and Colonel Crofby.

Serv. Colonel Crofby. [*Exit.*

Colonel. I hope I am not an intruder.—Blefs me, what has happened? Mifs Lydell in tears!

L. Kitty. Yes; the poor child has juft received a letter from her mother, one of the beft kind of women that ever was: Dry up your tears, Lydia, my love!—You fullen, fulk-

ing,

ing, ftomachful flut!—Poor Mrs. Lydell has but very bad health, Colonel Crofby; and the dear girl, who is indeed a moft affectionate dutiful daughter—Go up to your room, you pouting, perverfe, little vixen—You fee, Colonel! but be comforted, Lydy, my dear! though you fhould lofe your mother, you may be certain of finding a mother in me.

Colonel. I hope, Mifs, there is no immediate imminent danger.

L. Kitty. The poor child's tender nature, and amiable heart, makes her dread the worft that can happen.—What, is the wench petrified? move off, and don't ftand fniveling here!—She wifhes, Colonel, to withdraw to her chamber: But don't brood over your forrows, my love! order my coach, and take a little airing, my dear!—I hope it will overturn, and break every bone in your fkin.   [*Exit Lydia.*

Colonel. How amiable in your ladyfhip is this attention for fo deferving an object!

L. Kitty. I am afraid, Colonel, you will think it a weaknefs: Excefs of humanity is my foible, I know; but a generous mind, fuch as yours, Colonel, will pardon the error.

Colonel. Error! it is the glory, the pride of your fex; it is the invincible Ægis of Pallas, that muft fubdue every heart it attacks!

L. Kitty.

L. Kitty. Sorrows naturally foften the mind; and, Heaven knows, I have had a plentiful portion. The dear man, whofe refemblance I wear on my wrift——

Colonel. For Heaven's fake, madam——

L. Kitty. And for ever will wear—But what neceffity for this idle delufion? is not thy fweet image deeply graved in my heart?

Colonel. Indeed your ladyfhip fhould not give way to thefe tranfports; they may endanger your health.

L. Kitty. Look here! Can I then lament him too much?—But thou art but gone before me, my love!

Colonel. Let me refpect the facred hour of forrow, nor interrupt it by ufelefs confolation, and impertinent form! [*Exit.*

L. Kitty. A fhort fpace will unite us, never to bear the torture of feparation again! Oh, that it was permitted me, with my own hand to fhorten the time! this night, the arched vault fhould inclofe us! to the cold chamber of death I would with rapture defcend——

Enter Hetty.

How came that ill-bred puppy let in, without announcing his name?

Hetty.

Hetty. I fancy, Madam, the fervants were out of the way.

L. Kitty. That is always the cafe! Sure never was poor lady peftered by fuch an infamous fet! But you all know and take advantage of my patient and mild difpofition!

Hetty. To be fure, poor dove!—There are fome Englifh people below, beg to have the honour of feeing your ladyfhip.

L. Kitty. Do I know them?

Hetty. Mrs, Clack of Pall-Mall, with two or three more.

L. Kitty. Let Mrs. Clack firft be admitted. Is the room fit to receive them?

Hetty. Would your ladyfhip fee her in the Chamber of Tears?

L. Kitty. Where elfe? Light the candles, and fhut out the fun!   [_Exit Hetty._

This part that I play begins to grow horribly tedious. In my hufband's lifetime, indeed, I had one confolation at leaft, that I could always make him pay me in private for the good humour and fondnefs that I lavifhed on him in public: But now, I have no other refource but in fervants; and they too at times are rebellious. Thefe Englifh creatures get fuch odd notions about liberty into their heads! I fancy the Turks would make

good

good domeftics enough; but then the brutes
are fo tame and fubmiffive, that it is fcarce
poffible to teaze and torment them: Now the
great pleafure of power, is in ruling over fenfible fubjects, who wince and feel the yoke when
it galls them.—Blefs me! who is this?—Yes,
my lord, in thy tomb all my wifhes lie bur——

Enter Hetty.

Hetty. The room is ready, my lady.

L. Kitty. I wifh the room was on fire, and
you in the middle on't! plague on you! I
was afraid it was the Colonel come back.

[*Exeunt.*

A   C   T   III.

Enter Colonel Crofty.

Colonel.

THERE is a peculiarity in Mifs Lydell's diftrefs that I don't quite comprehend; it appears to arife from a deeper fource than Lady Kitty derives it. I wifh I could fee her ladyfhip's woman! The girl feems to have caught a good deal of the manners of her clafs in this country; curious, arch, and corrupt: With a proper application, there will be no difficulty, I fancy, to get at the family-fecrets.— Here fhe comes.

Enter Hetty.

You are in a prodigious hurry, Mrs. Hetty! Nothing uncommon has happened, I hope?

Hetty. Uncommon? no, no, Colonel; our affairs generally keep pretty much the fame train : Hurry-fcurry — fending — recalling — commanding—forbidding—Lord have mercy upon me! To live here, one fhould have the art of the Holloway-cheefecake-man, and be in a hundred places at the very fame time.

Colonel.

Colonel. She feems in a right cue for my purpofe.—You are upon no commiffion at prefent ?

Hetty. Not immediately; but I muft not be out
of the way ; for as my lady is deck'd out in
her difmals, perhaps fhe may take a fancy to
faint.

Colonel. Poor lady! Lady Kitty is, indeed,
a moft extraordinary inftance of the fincerity
and fervor of conjugal love.

Hetty. Yes; I believe there are very few
women can match her.

Colonel. And Mifs Lydell feems to have
caught the infection. How long, pray, has her
mother been fo exceedingly ill?

Hetty. Whofe mother?

Colonel. Mifs Lydell's.

Hetty. I never heard a word of her ficknefs.

Colonel. No! becaufe, my lady was——

Hetty. Yes; as I gueffed: This is one of
her tricks; fome ftory fhe has trump'd up.

Colonel. Indeed?—Oh, Mrs. Hetty; though
it is not ufual in this country to give vails, I
fuppofe you know it is the practice to pay fome
little occafional compliment, for the good offices
of thofe whom the injuftice of Fortune has
placed in a ftation below us.

Hetty. I have always faid, for politenefs, no
nation could equal the French.

Colonel.

Colonel. You will permit me to difcharge this
duty in part. [*Gives her money.*

Hetty. One may fee by your manner, Colonel,
where you have paffed the greateft part of your
time.

Colonel. I don't know any body's approbation
I am more ambitious to have.—But, Mrs.
Hetty; as to Mifs Lydell; there feems to be a
fixed melancholy hang on her brow.

Hetty. I don't wonder at it.

Colonel. But even now I furprized her in
tears.

Hetty. Like enough. I fuppofe fhe has been
under the lafh; my lady has been, as ufual, em-
ploying her talents in teazing.

Colonel. Talents in teazing?

Hetty. Yes; it is a little amufement her ladyfhip takes every morning, juft by way of exercife, between breakfaft and dinner.

Colonel. Oh, you wrong her ladyfhip! Indeed,
I never faw ftronger proofs of delicate and tender affection.

Hetty. Ha, ha! how eafily you men are impofed on!

Colonel. Nay, but, my dear girl, prithee don't
be fo giddy. To deal ferioufly with you, I
can't help taking a warm intereft in what relates
to Mifs Lydell.

K *Hetty.*

Hetty. Upon my word, fhe richly deferves it.

Colonel. And fhould be forry to find her prefent very alarming diftrefs owing to any indifcretion of hers.

Hetty. On that head, you may make yourfelf perfectly eafy.

Colonel. But how fhall we be able to account for——

Hetty. In the moft natural way in the world.

Colonel. Will you be kind enough to lend your affiftance?

Hetty. With all the pleafure in life. You can be fecret, I hope.

Colonel. You will find me a man of honour in every refpect.

Hetty. In one inftance, you have juft given me a convincing proof, I confefs. Why then, as to this lady of ours; in hypocrify fhe would be an over-match for a Methodift.

Colonel. Really?

Hetty. And as to cruelty, there never was fo ingenious, fo refined a tormentor: The Fathers of the Inquifition themfelves, would be proud to receive inftructions from her. I could give you fuch a hiftory——

Colonel. Is it poffible?

Hetty. This room is too public; befides, perhaps her ladyfhip may pop in and furprize **us,**

for

for she is as suspicious and prying as a custom-house officer. Dare you venture yourself in my room for a moment?

Colonel. If you are not apprehensive of danger, I must, Miss Hetty, be a coward indeed, if I——

Hetty. Oh, as to my own part, I know I am secure; you are engaged too deeply elsewhere.

Colonel. Me, child?

Hetty. Ha, ha, ha! Lord have mercy! how oddly you look! What, d'ye think I have not found you out before this? Nay, for the matter of that, my lady knows as much as myself; and, to tell you the truth, I believe that was the cause of the scene to which you were partly a witness.

Colonel. Nay, but, child——

Hetty. Hush! step into that room: I must introduce Mrs. Clack, the Mantua-maker, to an audience; after which, I'll be with you.

[*Exeunt.*

Lady Kitty discovered in deep mourning; the room hung with black; a lamp on the table.

L. Kitty. What the deuce keeps this woman so long? I grow most terribly tired of my attitude; but to this creature I must keep my character up: She is an absolute Gazette, and at

K 2   her

her return will publifh me in every part of the town.

Enter Hetty and Mrs. Clack.

Hetty. There you fee her ladyfhip fits; abforb'd in grief, quite abfent; fhe knows nothing of us.

Clack. Poor dear lady!

Hetty. I will endeavour to rouze her attention.

L. Kitty. Gone, loft, for ever loft!

Hetty. Pleafe your ladyfhip! madam!

L. Kitty. Why will you teaze me to fuftain a tedious life? I have no relifh for rich wines, or delicate viands; the bread of affliction is the beft banquet for me.

Clack. And that is but coarfe food, Heaven knows.

L. Kitty. Don't I hear fome other voice in the room? my eyes are grown fo mifty and dim——

Hetty. With crying!—Mrs. Clack, your ladyfhip's mantua-maker, from England, to pay her duty; and defires your ladyfhip's commands for that country.

L. Kitty. Let her approach.—How d'ye do, Mrs. Clack?—Hetty, child, you may go to your dinner.—A good creature; an humble kind of friend, Mrs. Clack: To her care and attention

tention I think myfelf deeply indebted; as fhe will find when they open my will.

Hetty. For Heaven's fake! your ladyfhip makes my blood run cold in my veins.

L. Kitty. D'ye think, Hetty, you fhall lament me?

Hetty. Can your ladyfhip doubt it? I fhould almoft break my heart, if your ladyfhip was not to leave me a farthing.

L. Kitty. Should you? Kind foul!—I fhall try the experiment, you hypocritical flut!

Hetty. But when our fuperiors are fo con-fiderate as to think of their menials in their laft moments, to be fure it gives poor fervants greater fpirits to cry for their lofs.

L. Kitty. Doubtlefs. You may go. [*Exit Hetty.* Well, Mrs. Clack, you find me vaftly altered fince the death of Sir John.

Clack. To be fure, your ladyfhip is fome-thing changed fince the day I had the honour to try on your ladyfhip's cloaths for your ladyfhip's wedding.

L. Kitty. True. You, I think, Mrs. Clack, decked me out like another Iphigenia, to be facrificed at the temple of Hymen. Don't you recollect the tremors, the terrors, that in-vaded each nerve, on that folemn, that awful occafion? You muft remember, with what re-

luctance

luctance I was dragged by Sir John to the altar.

Clack. To be fure, your ladyfhip fhewed a becoming coynefs upon the occafion. I remember, about the hour of bedding, you hid yourfelf behind the bottle-rack in the beer-cellar, to avoid Sir John; if your ladyfhip had not happened to have coughed, we fhould not have found you.

L. Kitty. The conflict was great: But, dear Mrs. Clack, what could I do? Troy ftood a fiege for only ten years; now fixteen were fully accomplifhed before I was compelled to furrender.

Clack. That was ftanding out a vaft while, to be fure. I recollects, what added to your ladyfhip's grief was, that the nuptials fhould happen to fall out in the middle of Lent.

L. Kitty. Dear Clack, you renew my confufion: Little did I think ever to fully that facred feafon, by the celebration of fuch a feftivity. \

Clack. But there could not be fo much harm in the matter neither, as marriages, your ladyfhip knows, are all fettled above.

L. Kitty. By that argument I was induced to furrender; with, however, an exprefs ftipulation, that all connubial intercourfe fhould be fufpended Wednefdays and Fridays.

Clack.

Clack. That muſt have been a vaſt denial to both parties, no doubt.

L. Kitty. How, Mrs. Clack! you wou'dn't in-ſinuate that I was prompted to the connection by any——

Clack. Far from it, my lady! I only meant, that it muſt give your ladyſhip pain to refuſe Sir John any favour; for, to be ſure, never was any lady half ſo happy in a partner as you.

L. Kitty. How irreparable muſt then be my loſs! Yes, Clack, he poſſeſs'd my whole heart, and poſſeſſes it ſtill : My waking thoughts are all devoted to him; in ſleep his lov'd image is ever before me—ſtarting from my couch,

" I cry aloud; he hears not what I ſay :
" I ſtretch my empty arms; he glides away !"

Clack. Vaſt mournful indeed ! But I ſhould think your ladyſhip might find out a cure.

L. Kitty. Which way ?

Clack. Fill your empty arms with ſomething ſubſtantial, and I warrant 'twill frighten the phantom.

L. Kitty. Clack, I don't comprehend——

Clack. I only recommends to your lady-ſhip the proſcription I made uſe on myſelf: There was my firſt huſband, ſweet Mr. Snip, though a ſtaymaker, as portly a perſon—I really believes,

believes, I fhould have followed the dear foul to his grave, hadn't our foreman, Tom Clack, ftep'd in to confole me; indeed, the match was very convenient, as he had done all my hufband's bufinefs during the time of his ficknefs.

L. Kitty. I am aftonifh'd, woman, at your prefumption. Do you recollect to whom you are addreffing this language?

Clack. I beg pardon! But I thought in thefe matters your ladyfhip was like the reft of our fex; and though Sir John——

L. Kitty. Peace! nor let your unhallow'd lips profane the dear name! even now, his facred fhade feems to upbraid me: See there!

Clack. There? where? I fees nothing, I'm fure.

L. Kitty. How awful, how tremendous, he looks! his front furrow'd, for the firft time, with a frown!

Clark. Lord blefs me! I wifh I was well out of the houfe!

L. Ketty. But, be pacified, dear lord of my life; no fecond to thee fhall fucceed:

" Firft let the opening earth a paffage rend,
" And let me thro' the dark abyfs defcend,
" Before I break the plighted faith I gave!
" Thou hadft my vows, and fhalt for ever have;
" For whom I lov'd on earth, I'll worfhip in the grave!"

Clack.

Clack. Never ftir, if fhe ben't talking of poetry! her brain's turn'd, to be fure.

L. Kitty.. He beckons! lead on, my lov'd lord! thy fummons I with rapture obey. His arms encircle me round; and now together we plunge into the gulph! the raging billows furround us! now they rife o'er our heads! now we fink, we fink, in filence together! and, oh—[*falling.*] Curfe the chair! how came I to mifs it?

Clack. Mercy upon us! help, for Heaven's fake, help! What, is there nobody left in the houfe?

Enter Hetty.

Lord, Mrs. Hetty, I am glad you are come! My poor lady! fhe is quite gone, I am afraid.

Hetty. On the ground! in one of her fits, I fuppofe.—No doubt, it is dreadful to you; but we are us'd to 'em every day. Step and call fome more of the—[*Exit Clack.*] How came your ladyfhip to fall on the ground?

L. Kitty. Where the deuce have you been? that old fool was fo frighted, fhe never thought of bringing the chair. She has pinch'd me as black as a coal.

Hetty. Would your ladyfhip pleafe to recover now, or fhall I fetch in the hartfhorn?

L   *L. Kitty.*

L. Kitty. This woman is an ideot; fo there is no occafion at prefent.

Hetty. Come back, Mrs. Clack; my lady begins to revive,

Re-enter Mrs. Clack.

and upon thefe occafions fhe wifhes to have but few people by. T'other fide, Mrs. Clack. So, fo, fo!

L. Kitty. Am I recall'd to hated life again?

Hetty. Your ladyfhip has had a violent ftruggle. Nothing more than ufual, I hope, has happened.

Clack. I believes indeed it was partly my fault: In order to comfort my lady, I was rafh enough to recommend another huf——

L. Kitty. Recal not the detefted idea, unlefs you wifh to fee me fink again at your feet!

Clack. I beg your ladyfhip's pardon! I can't think what in the world could poffefs me! Indeed, Lord Harry Huntwidow, hearing that I was going over, did defire me to deliver a letter.

L. Kitty. To me? prefumptuous man! how dar'd he encourage a hope——Had not he heard that Don Juan de Muftachio, a Spanifh grandee of the very firft clafs, had laid his Golden Fleece at my feet?

Hetty.

Hetty. True enough.

L. Kitty. Didn't the Palfgrave of Saltfplafh, a fovereign Prince on the banks of the Rhine, offer to fhare his power with me? and, after all, to fubmit to a fubject!—This Lord Harry, Hetty, is an abfolute beggar: Red-faced, rabbet-back'd, with a pair of legs like a couple of drumfticks.

Hetty. Marry come up, my fcurvy companion!

Clack. As foon as ever I return, I fhall deliver his lordfhip his letter.

L. Kitty. Hold, Clack; let it lie on the table.

Clack. Will your ladyfhip deign then to give it a reading?

L. Kitty. By no means, Mrs. Clack. Put it amongft the other papers, Hetty, which in a few days are to expire in the flames.

Hetty. It fhall, Madam.

L. Kitty. A monthly facrifice I offer up, Mrs. Clack, before the dear image of him I adore.

Hetty. We fhall have a fine blaze; for this month has been very prolific.—My lady's illnefs had made me like to forget; your relations, Mrs. Clack, grow impatient without.

L. Kitty. Who are they?

Clack. A fifter of mine, and her hufband, to beg your ladyfhip's intereft to get their daughter out of a convent.

L 2   *L. Kitty.*

L. Kitty. A convent! how got she there?

Clack. Run away from her parents, with a paltry 'prentice, to avoid the man of their chufing; an' purtends, on purpofe to plague 'em, that she wants to be a nun; and, what is worfer, threatens to turn Papifh if they torment her.

L. Kitty. Of what ufe can I be?

Clack. If your ladyfhip could order the child to be deliver'd back to her parents——

L. Kitty. This is a matter of weight, Mrs. Clack, and muft be confidered maturely: I am too ill, at prefent, to admit an audience. I fhall defire the governor to direct a guard to efcort your niece to my prefence; we fhall then fee what is beft to be done. Hetty, let the governor know my defire. But this, Mrs. Clack, I muft tell you; if the girl's converfion is the matter in queftion, I can on no account interpofe; the friendfhip I have with the Pope ties my hands where the Holy See is concern'd.

Clack. Nothing of that, believe me, my lady.

L. Kitty. But don't indulge a furmife, which was circulated, even at Rome itfelf, with too much fuccefs, that any thing fenfual tainted the intercourfe between the reverend Pontiff and me.

Clack. Heaven forbid that I fhould think of any fuch thing!

L. Kitty. Malice, join'd with credulity, gave

rife

rife to the fable : Sacred fentiments, that fpring in kindred minds, firft began and cemented the union. Every avenue, but what friendfhip permits, is guarded by thy lov'd image, my lord ! thou, who art the alphabet, the beginning, the ending, the very Great A and Z, of all my tender affections.   [*Exit.*

Clack. Poor lady ! fhe is in a piteous plight ; for all the world like Mrs. Andromedy, that one fees at the theatre.

Hetty. Ay, Mrs. Clack ; to all widows fhe is indeed a fhining example.

Clack. True. Why, I myfelf, if my hufband had left me in circumftances accordingly, fhould have taken on a great deal more than I did ; but folks, who have their living to get, can't afford to cry, you know, as much as your people of fafhion ; befides, every body has not the gift of incontinence, like to my lady.

Hetty. True, true. But you had better ftep out to your friends, and let them know what meafures my lady has taken.

Clack. I will, I will ; they will be impatient, no doubt.   [*Exit.*

Hetty. Colonel, you may appear.

Enter Colonel.

Well, Sir, after what you have feen and heard, I fuppofe all your doubts are remov'd.

Colonel.

Colonel. Perfectly fatisfied; a new edition of the Ephefian Matron, with amazing improvements. But poor Mifs Lydell! I own her fituation diftreffes me greatly.

Hetty. The damfel, it is true, is in terrible durance : Do you feel yourfelf knight-errant enough to fly to her refcue?

Colonel. Would the lady, d'ye think, accept of my fervice?

Hetty. It is but a poor compliment to fuppofe that fhe wou'dn't prefer the foft bondage of love, to the galling fetters fhe wears.

Colonel. Can I then, Mrs. Hetty, hope for nothing more than a preference?

Hetty. I don't think myfelf at liberty, Colonel, to tell you all that I know. In the drawing-room, you will find the young lady alone: As you gave me a handfome retainer, I have been in court and open'd the caufe; do you fpeak to the merits; you are a good pleader, and I make no doubt will fucceed.

Colonel. I will go and labour hard for a verdict.

Hetty. You will find the court inclined to your fuit. But, Colonel, you have no objections, when you have delivered the damfel, to break the chains of her confidante too?

Colonel. The romance would be irregular elfe. [*Exit.*

Hetty. So! her ladyfhip's power draws towards a period;

a period; fhe muft provide new fubjects, at leaft. She fuppofed the hopes from her Will would fecure me; but the day is too diftant; befides, I know her too well to have any reliance—

Enter Servant.

Serv. Blefs me, Mrs. Hetty, what can be the matter? Here is a file of mufqueteers coming into the houfe.

Hetty. The girl, I fuppofe, from the convent. A new whim of my lady's: I will go to them; you have nothing to fear. [*Exeunt.*

Scene changes to another Apartment.

Enter Mr. and Mrs. Minnikin, and Codling.

Mrs. Min. Now, fon Codling, boldly put in your claim. We will fupport you, I warrant.

Enter Mrs. Clack.

Well, fifter, what news from my lady?

Clack. Small hopes, I am afraid: The gentlewoman herfelf is in a defperate taking; but Jenny will be forth-coming, however. I fancy here fhe is, by the noife on the ftairs.

Enter Lapelle.

Lap. Serviture, Monfieurs and Mefdames!—— Why, what the deuce is the matter? There is
your

your daughter below, furrounded by a troop of *foldas*, as the French call them.—Here fhe is.

Enter Jenny and foldiers.

Mrs. Min. So, Jenny! You fee what you have brought yourfelf to, to be made a fhow on in the ftreets, guarded like a——

Jenny. I am not the firft, Madam, who has fuffered for the fake of Religion.

Mrs. Min. Religion? Rebellion, you hypo-critical flut!

Jenny. Can I give a ftronger proof of my fincerity, than in quitting a life of affluence and eafe, to embrace poverty, fafting, and penance?

Min. Not one of the three, but thee wouldft run twenty miles to avoid! No, no, Jenny, that's all a pretence; it is not poverty, but fomething elfe, you want to embrace.

Lap. Hold, Monfieur Minnikin! You are a little too hafty: *Jeunes filles,* as the French fay, are not to be treated fo roughly; fuffer me to *parle un pew.* Is it true, *Madamoifelle, mon amy* Codling, becaufe you are *amorew* of fomebody elfe——

Jenny. My duty, Sir, directs me not to con-tradict what a father affirms.

Min. Yes, yes, you are plaguy dutiful all of a fudden!

Clack.

Clack. Hufh! Here comes my lady; leave the matter to her.

Enter Lady Kitty and Hetty.

L. Kitty. Hetty, order the guards to with-draw. [*Exe. Sold.*]—Which are the parties? and what their caufe of complaint?

Min. Why, pleafe your ladyfhip, our bufinefs is this: That young flut that ftands there, who, between ourfelves, for all her fanctified looks—

L. Kitty. Honeft friend, you are too familiar and loud.

Lap. Hufh, Matt! and let me open the mat-ter.—Matt Minnikin, my lady, an honeft *bur-goife*, that lives *dans* the *citè*, won't fet fire to the Thames, though he lives near the Bridge; a namefake, but no relation to Mr. *Mat-Chavel*—

L. Kitty. You too are pretty forward, I think! And, pray, Sir, who and what may you be?

Lap. *Per vous fervice*, as the French fay, my name is Lapelle; by diftraction, a Frenchman, though a native of *Londre*; my purdeceffors were mefugees, and came over after the revolu-tion of the edict of Nantz. Don't you think, my lady, there is a *quelque chofe* in my manner, a fomething, that fpeaks me fprung from the French?

M   *L. Kitty.*

L. Kitty. Rather more relative in your modesty, Mr. Lapelle.

Lap. Powteter, my lady.

L. Kitty. But let this honeſt man tell his own ſtory; he ſeems very able.

Lap. With all my heart; *de tout mon cur,* as the French ſay.—Come, Matthew! *alons!*

Min. Why, I ſay, my lady, as I was ſaying, that girl there——

Lap. Pardy affes ſhenteel; and, for an Engliſh face, a pretty jolly viſage enough.

L. Kitty. Peace, Sir!

Lap. My lady, *pardunn!*

Min. Rather, I ſay, than marry this honeſt neighbour of ours, as reputable a tradeſ——

Lap. Ceſt vrais; Monſieur Codling lives in *beaucope de credit.*

L. Kitty. Nobody called on you as a voucher.

Lap. Aſſurement, my lady.

Min. She has run away along with our 'prentice; but as we followed pretty cloſe at their heels, not having time to complete their projeᵭ, ſhe has taken refuge here in a convent; and ſays, moreover, if we perſiſts, ſhe will promiſcuouſly turn Papiſh and Nun.

Lap. Pour a Papiſh, *powteter;* but *pour la* nun, *pardonnez moi!* my lady, *que dities vous?*

L. Kitty. Will nobody ſilence this impertinent

nent jackanapes ?—Well, child, you hear what
your father alleges.

Jenny. May I crave your ladyfhip's private
ear for a moment ?

L. Kitty. Withdraw; not out of the room.
—Well, child; what are the objections to the
man your parents have chofen ?

Jenny. Two as ftrong ones as any mortal can
have : I hate him, and I love another.

L. Kitty. Pretty frank, I muft own.—And
as to the change of religion——

Jenny. A mere fetch, to keep out of their
hands.

L. Kitty. You have no hopes that your parents
will yield ?

Jenny. Mother, perhaps, might comply; but
no mule is fo headftrong as father.

L. Kitty. And you, I fuppofe, are as deter-
min'd as he ?

Jenny. Never once gave up a point in my life.

L. Kitty. I dare fay. But, if they were to
defire you to marry the 'prentice——

Jenny. They would find me a dutiful daughter.

L. Kitty. Then you have no objection to obey
their commands, when they happen to contain
the very things that you wifh ?

Jenny. Not in the leaft.

L. Kitty. And after having produced, and at

M 2   their

their own expence trained and fuftained you, you would ftill fuffer them, I dare fay, to fupport and protect you?

Jenny. As in duty they are bound.

L. Kitty. And they might direct you, provided you govern'd them?

Jenny. In every refpect.

L. Kitty. Well faid, my little American! you would be an heroine, child, on the other fide the Atlantic. Why, in your cafe, Mifs Jenny, I don't fee what we can do: There is, indeed, one expedient, if you find you have courage enough to perform it.

Jenny. I fhall not flinch, my lady, when it comes to the pufh.

L. Kitty. There are, my dear, two men who folicit your hand; one favour'd by you, the other your father approves.

Jenny. My fituation exactly.

L. Kitty. Suppofe then, by way of reconciling all parties, you were to marry 'em both?

Jenny. The happieft thought in the world! I wonder it never came into my head.—But, I am afraid, my lady, we have not dignity enough to do fuch a thing as this without danger.

L. Kitty. We will confider of this at our leifure.—How fhould you like living with me in this town?

Jenny.

Jenny. Of all things upon earth.

L. Kitty. We will fee what can be done.—
Mr. and Mrs. Minnikin, I have been founding
your daughter; a little time and fome proper
perfuafions, may induce her to comply with
your wifhes.

Mrs. Min. We are highly indebted to your
ladyfhip's goodnefs!

L. Kitty. One of my maids of honour is returning to England; I fhall have no objection
to promoting Mrs. Clack's niece to the place.

Clack. Brother Minnikin!—We fhall be bound
to pray for your ladyfhip.

L. Kitty. Here Lydia comes, and the Colonel
clofe with her!

Enter Colonel and Lydia.

Lydia, my dear, though with the greateft re-
gret, yet the defign is fo laudable, I confent
that you may return to your mother; thefe
honeft people, my love, will conduct you with
care.

Colonel. My Lydia, Madam, will not want
their affiftance.

L. Kitty. Colonel? I don't underftand you.

Colonel. That honour I propofe having
myfelf.

L. Kitty. How, Colonel!—Shall I crave a
word?

word ? I hope you have no bad defigns on the girl.

Colonel. None but fuch as I hope her friends will approve ?

L. Kitty. Is it poffible you can be in earneft ?

Colonel. What fhould make your ladyfhip doubt it ?

L. Kitty. Indeed ? Nay, if that be the cafe, it would be criminal in me to conceal a fecret in which your honour is concerned : Thofe tears, which my humanity made me attribute to her filial fears for her mother, flow'd from a more ignoble fource.

Colonel. How, Madam !

L. Kitty. A love, perhaps, for one of my menials. How far it proceeded, I fha'n't take upon me to fay ; but, to avoid fcandal, I found myfelf obliged to difcard him.

Colonel. Ha, ha ! what a happy invention !

L. Kitty. I don't underftand you.

Colonel. Why, to deal with your ladyfhip plainly, your addrefs is ill employ'd upon me : I own it confummate ; but I have been a con-ceal'd witnefs to fome of your arts, and fhall hardly be impofed on again. Come, Mifs Ly-dia ; you will take leave of her ladyfhip : Her paft favours may foon be acknowledg'd.

L. Kitty. Is this true, Lydia ?

Mifs L.

Miss L. Your ladyfhip's approbation, on an event fo honourable and advantageous for me, I make no doubt of obtaining.

L. Kitty. Is it poffible that you can quit my protection, and throw yourfelf into the arms of a renegade?

Colonel. How, Madam!

L. Kitty. Was not your father a rebel?

Colonel. True, Madam.

L. Kitty. And a'n't you an officer in the fervice of France?

Colonel. I was, Madam; but my prefent royal mafter, who is above the narrow prejudice of punifhing the principles of parents in their unfortunate offspring, has accepted my fervice, and reftored my family to the rights of their country. For that fpot I fhall embark in the morning; leaving your ladyfhip to lament the lofs of a fubject to exercife your mifchief and malice upon; which I fancy you will more heavily mifs, notwithftanding your weeds, than the poor knight who was happy, though even by death, to efcape from fo unfeeling a tyrant!

L. Kitty. Barbarous, inhuman monfter! how dare you recal the memory of the dear—had' he lived, thus to fee me infulted—but that could not have been; Thou wouldft never have

borne

borne it, my love!—but I am rightly punifh'd, for fuffering even a thought to be diverted from thee !—Hetty, lead to my clofet, there to com- pofe my ruffled——

Hetty. Pleafe your ladyfhip, I muft beg to be excus'd ; I am engag'd to take on with Mifs Lydy.

L. Kitty. Is it fo ? well, well ! You will fol- low me with your niece. You fee in me, Mrs. Clack, another Darius, deferted at my utmoft need, by thofe my former bounty fed. But, what have I to do with mankind ? all my wifhes and wants lie beyond them ! I defire no com- panion but thee :

" Whilft on thy form I fix my eager eyes,
" The world I laugh at, and its threats defpife." [*Exit.*

Colonel. The world will be even with your ladyfhip, or I am greatly miftaken.—Come, my love, it is time to prepare for our voyage.

Lap. You are bound, Colonel, for *Angleterre*, as the French call it ?

Colonel. By the very firft fhip.

Lap. I wonder that you, who have refided fo long in France, can bear the thoughts of living at London.

Colonel. It is that very circumftance that will give it an additional relifh : And believe this,

master

Mafter Lapelle, as a truth; no man ever yet deferted his country, unlefs he had previoufly been by that country deferted. : . i .. ..

Lap. Commong can that be? *permitte moi* to laugh, as they fay: You fee how this town is crouded with *Anglois*.

Colonel. Too true, I confefs; and particularly, Mafter Lapelle, by thofe of your bufinefs; who, at the fame time that they are exclaiming in every paper againft the importation of French manufactures, have engrofs'd almoft the whole of that part of the fmuggling trade to themfelves. I dare fay, you are at prefent furnifh'd with a pretty good cargo.

Lap. To oblige fome *my lors*, who are my particular friends, I can't fay——

Colonel. Nay, be cautious how you truft me with your fecrets! there may be fome danger.—— Come, Mifs; in this houfe we have nothing further to do.

Mifs L. I can't fay, but I feel fome concern for the young victim Lady Kitty has juft got into her power.

Hetty. You may difcard your fears about her! unlefs I am miftaken, they are very properly match'd, and will prove a mutual plague to each other. But, fhould it be otherwife, there feems to be a kind of dramatic juftice in the

N   change

change of your two fituations : You, Mifs, are rewarded for your patient fufferings, by the protection of a man of honour and virtue ; whilft fhe, rebellious to the mild dictates of parental fway, is fubjected to the galling yoke of a capricious and whimfical tyrant!

END of the TRIP TO CALAIS.

THE

C A P U C H I N;

A C O M E D Y,

IN THREE ACTS.

AS IT IS PERFORMED AT THE

THEATRE-ROYAL in the HAYMARKET.

ALTERED FROM

THE TRIP TO CALAIS,

BY THE LATE

S A M U E L F O O T E, *Esq.*

AND NOW PUBLISHED BY

Mr. C O L M A N.

THE
CAPUCHIN;
A COMEDY,
IN THREE ACTS;

P R O L O G U E.

Written by Mr. C O L M A N.

Spoken by Mr. F O O T E.

CRITICS, whene'er I write, in every scene
Discover meanings that I never mean :
Whatever character I bring to view,
I am the father of the child, 'tis true,
But every babe his chrift'ning owes to you.
" The comic poet's eye," with humorous air,
Glancing from Watling-Street to Grofvenor-Square,
He bodies forth a light ideal train,
And turns to shape the phantoms of his brain ;
Meanwhile, your fancy takes more partial aim,
" And gives to airy nothing place and name."
    A limner once, in want of work, went down
To try his fortune in a country town ;
The waggon, loaded with his goods, convey'd
To the fame spot his whole dead ftock in trade ;
Originals, and copies—ready made.
To the new painter all the country came ;
Lord, lady, doctor, lawyer, fquire, and dame,
The humble curate, and the curate's wife,
All afk a likenefs—taken from the life.
Behold the canvas on the eafel ftand !
A pallet grac'd his thumb, and brufhes fill'd his hand ;
But, ah ! the painter's fkill they little knew,
Nor by what curious rules of art he drew.
The waggon-load unpack'd, his ancient ftore
Furnifh'd for each a face drawn long before ;
God, dame, or hero cf the days of yore.

                                                    The

The Cæfars, with a little alteration,
Were turn'd into the mayor and corporation;
To reprefent the rector and the dean,
He added wigs and bands to prince Eugene;
The ladies, blooming all, deriv'd their faces
From Charles the Second's beauties, and the Graces.
   Thus done, and circled in a fplendid frame,
His works adorn'd each room, and fpread his fame.
The country Men of Tafte admire and ftare,
" My lady's leer! Sir John's majeftic air!
" Mifs Dimple's languifh too! extremely like!
" And in the ftile and manner of Vandyke!—
" Oh! this new limner's pictures always ftrike.
" Old, young, fat, lean, dark, fair, or big or little,
" The very man or woman to a tittle!"
   Foote and this limner in fome points agree;
And thus, good Sirs, you often deal by Me.
When, by the royal licence and protection,
I fhew my fmall academy's collection,
The connoiffeur takes out his glafs, to pry
Into each picture with a curious eye;
Turns topfy-turvy my whole compofition,
And makes mere portraits all my exhibition.
   From various forms Apelles Venus drew:
So from the million do I copy you.
" But ftill the copy's fo exact," you fay:
Alas! the fame thing happens every day!
How many a modifh, well-drefs'd fop you meet,
Exactly fuits his fhape in Monmouth-Street.
In Yorkfhire warehoufes and Cranbourn-Alley,
'Tis wonderful how fhoes and feet will tally!
As honeft Crifpin underftands his trade,
On the true human fcale his lafts are made;

PROLOGUE.

The meafure of each fex and age to hit,
And every fhoe, as if befpoke, will fit.
  My warehoufe, thus, for Nature's walks, fupplies
Shoes for all ranks, and lafts of every fize.
Sit ftill and try 'em, Sirs; I long to pleafe you:
How well they fit! I hope you find 'em eafy!
If the fhoe pinches, fwear you cannot bear it;
But, if well made, I wifh you health to wear it!

DRAMATIS

DRAMATIS PERSONÆ.

Sir Harry Hamper,	*Mr. Parsons.*
Doctor Viper,	*Mr. Palmer.*
O'Donnovan,	*Mr. Foote.*
Colonel,	*Mr. L'Estrange.*
Mr. Minnikin,	*Mr. Edwin.*
Kit Codling,	*Mr. Bannister.*
Dick Drugget,	*Mr. R. Palmer.*
Tromfort,	*Mr. Baddeley.*
La Jeunesse,	
Peter Packthread,	
Kit Cable,	

Postillions, Porters, Shoe-Blacks, &c.

Mrs. Minnikin,	*Miss Sherry.*
Mrs. Clack,	*Miss Platt.*
Jenny Minnikin,	*Mrs. Jewell.*
Abbess.	*Mrs. Love.*
Nun.	

THE

CAPUCHIN.

[*In order to avoid swelling the bulk, and encreasing
the Price, of these Pieces, such Passages in* the
Capuchin *as are exactly similar to those in* the
Trip to Calais, *are not reprinted; but the Reader
is referred to the Pages in which the Dialogue
and Fable connect the two Dramas.*]

A C T   I.

[*The first variation from* the Trip to Calais *is by
the following insertion, after* Tromfort's *speech
ending,* " for he is ver fond of de fea," *p.* 9.]

Tromfort.

SOME littel time paft, ve vas have an-
oder gentleman of de fame kind in dis
town : He vas a *grand* autere ; *diable,*
a man of great deal of vit, *beaucoup
d' efprit.*

Jenny. Ay ?

O

Tromf.

Tromf. Oh, *oui!* he vas write de pretty paragraph in de Gazette, vat you call your news-
paper? by gar, he lay about him like *le diable!*
Poff, poff, poff! he make all de my lors, ay, and
my ladies too, fhake in dere two fhoe.

Dick. What brought him here?

Tromf. He vas come over here vid my lady
Deborah Dripping.

Jenny. Is her ladyfhip here?

Tromf. No; fhe vas go to Italy to vifit de Pope.

Dick. And leave the Doctor behind?

Tromf. You know he vas Proteftant *Pretre:*
Not but he vas ver polite, and offered to turn
Papift, to vait on de lady.

Dick. That was very complaifant of the Doctor.
Where is he now?

Tromf. He is gone governeur to fhew dis country to a chevalier *Anglois,* an Englifh knight, I
dink dey call, Sir Harry de Hamper.

[*The Dialogue is then continued without any variation to p. 22; where, inftead of the entrance of
Lapelle, Gingham, and La Jeuneffe, the Act was
continued, and concluded, as follows.*]

Mrs. Min. Blefs me, what a rumbling is that!

Re-enter Codling.

Codl. I fancy, an old neighbour of yours,
that has juft drove into the yard.

Min.

Min. Who can it be?

Codl. Mafter Hamper, that kept the great tea-fhop at the corner of Cornhill; you remember him?

Min. What fhould ail me? many a tiff have we taken at Mother Red-Cap's, in our Sunday-nights' walks up to Hampftead.

Mrs. Min. Ay, but, Matt, times are altered with him now: Since the death of his brother, he is become a knight banneret, and perhaps may chufe to forget his old friends.

Min. Ay, ay, like enough. Upon his coming to his means, he grew too proud to live in the City; fo fhut up fhop, and I ha'n't got fight of him fince. Son Codling, doft know what brought him here?

Clack. Sir Harry Hamper! is he here? I fhall be happy to fee him; I had the honour to furnifh him with fome tom-bore waiftcoats when he fet out on his tower.

Min. Tower! what a deuce could provoke him to leave home?

Clack. Wanted to fee the world, I fuppofe.

Min. See the world? what, juft as he is going out on't?

: *Clack.* And to qualify him for the honour of a young lady of quality's hand, that lives in our Square, to whom he paid his addreffes; but fhe nfifts upon his polifhing a little.

Min. A young lady? what, Harry Hamper? Zounds, why, he is ten years older than I am! on the wrong fide of feventy, I'll be upon oath.

Clack. Ay, that is as you reckon him; but he dates his birth from the day of his fucceeding to the family honours.

Mrs. Min. About five years ago.

Min. He is not far from the mark; once a man, and twice a child!

Coal. To my thinking, thefe mounfeers have disfigured him ftrangely; if it had not been for Peter Packthread, his old fhopman, whom he keeps as his valet de fham, I fhould never have known him.

Min. I reckon he is as proud as Old Nick.

Coal. I can't fay much as to that. Peter fays that his mafter has not pick'd up much of their lingo, fo his fpeech is pretty much as it was; he talks to every body, runs from one thing to t'other, and rattles away at his old rate, I can tell you.

Mrs. Min. But how does he manage to call for fuch things as he wants?

Codl. He pick'd up a clargyman, as he pafs'd thro' this town, and carried him with him, as his travelling tuterer. Oh, here he is.

Enter

Enter Sir Harry Hamper, Peter Packthread, Dr. Viper, and Two Postillions.

Sir H. Come, come! come along, Doctor! Peter, give the postillions thirty soufes a-piece.

Peter. 'Tis put down, they are to have but five, in the book.

Sir H. No matter; it will let them know we are somebody, Peter.

Peter. What significations that? ten to one, we shall never see them again.

Sir H. Do as you are bid! [*Peter pays the Post.*

Peter. There! Pox take 'em, see how they grin! ay, ay, I dare be sworn you ha'n't seen such a sum this many a day.

1st Post. Serviteur! bonne voyage, Monsieur my lor!   [*Exeunt Post.*

Sir H. There, there, Peter! my lord! I have purchased a title for ten-pence; that is dog-cheap, or the devil's in't!

Peter. Nay, in that respect, the folks here make but little difference between their dogs and your worship, I think; for every mangy cur I have met with, is either *prince*, or *my lord*, or *marquis*.

Clack. I am happy to see your honour in France.

Sir H. What, Mrs. Clack! and Master Minnikin and wife, as I live! How fares it, my old City friends?

Min.

Min. Thank you, thank you, Sir Harry! What, you have been the grand tower, I fuppofe.

Sir H. Ay, Matt: What's money without manners? I have enough of the firft, to be fure; and I wanted to fee if I could not pick up a little of the laft.

Clack. And how does your honour like France?

Sir H. Only the firft fpot in the world, Mrs. Clack: For eating, drinking, laughing, and loving, *vive la France!* hey, Domine?

Mrs. Min. Eating! fure your honour does not think their wictuals are better than our'n.

Sir H. Wictuals! Lord help your roaft-beef and plumb-pudding foul! why, there are no fuch things in the country.

Min. No! I have heard, indeed, they had not over much plenty; but I didn't think the poor creatures were fo bad off as that.

Sir H. What, becaufe a whole family does not get round a fir-loin of beef, or a faddle of mutton, and devour it like a kennel of hounds! Can there be any thing fo favage, as to eat up fheep and oxen like a parcel of cannibals: I wonder they don't drefs them in their fleece and their hides; hey, Domine!

Viper. Doubtlefs, Sir Harry, the French elegance would never be able to digeft fuch grofs animal food in its natural form; he therefore is the beft cook with them who can difguife it the beft,

Mrs.

Mrs. Min. Indeed?

Sir H. To be fure. Why, except a fide dish
of ftew'd fnails, or fome fricafeed frogs, I haven't
known the name of any thing I have tafted fince
I came over.

Min. Lord have mercy upon us!—And
as to love, Sir Harry, I fhould think that was
pretty near over with you.

Sir H. Domine, did you ever hear fuch a
blockhead!—Why, fool, it was my own fault,
or I might have gone into keeping.

Min. Into keeping? you?

Sir H. Me! afk Domine only. What was
the name of the duchefs?

Viper. What fignifies naming of one? there
was not a day, that I didn't receive feveral
commiffions of a fimilar nature.

Mrs. Min. Indeed?

Sir H. Domine Viper receiv'd the letters,
and us'd to read 'em to me in Englifh.

Viper. They at laft became fo exceedingly
troublefome, that I was oblig'd to recommend
to Sir Harry the entertaining an Opera girl, in
order to convince them that they had miftaken
their man; and that fo far from receiving, we
were able to pay.

Sir H. And fo he got me Mademoifelle Mouche,
a fweet lovely fyren; and the little rogue was fo
excellively

exceffively fond, Domine Viper thinks fhe will hardly furvive my departure.

Min. Wonderful!

Sir H. Fell into 'ftericks at my going off in the chay; didn't fhe? fo I left Domine to confole her a little; but you found the way to make her eafy at laft.

Viper. A difficult job.

Sir H. I had fome thoughts of carrying her over to England, and taking a box for her at the Opera during the feafon; but I thought it might give offence in a certain quarter that you know, Mrs. Clack.

Clack. There might have been fome danger in that.

Sir H. Otherwife, Mademoifelle, the Doctor, and I, fhould have made a fweet *tête-à-tête* on the road.

Min. I reckon fhe muft a' coft you a power of money.

Sir H. Coft? that's always uppermoft in a citizen's mouth: Not a farthing, you fool! I am fure, fhe would have quitted me, if I had but made her the offer. Domine!

Viper. Oh! mere paffion; not an idea of intereft.

Sir H. Domine heard, indeed, by accident, fhe had contracted fome debts to fupport her relations, for fhe is the beft creature on earth;

and

and wanted vaftly to have a fmall fervice of plate, and fome ear-rings.

Mrs. Min. Which you gave her, I reckon?

Sir H. Not I: I was oblig'd to get Domine to manage the bufinefs. Had fhe had the leaft fufpicion of me, there would have been the devil to pay; we fhould have all been off in an inftant.

Mrs. Min. The Doƈtor has, I find, been very ufeful to you, Sir Harry.

Sir H. Could have done nothing without him: Not a week ago, he got me out of a devilifh fcrape.

Min. How?

Sir H. Got to picquet with a count, a great man of the Doƈtor's acquaintance; I can't fay, I know much of the game; but what of that? one wou'dn't appear ignorant amongft the French, you know, for the honour of England.

Clack. Oh fy! by no means.

Sir H. Egod, the count gave me a trimming; loft a devilifh deal more than I had in the country; but Domine made it up for me, among his acquaintance, upon my only giving my note.

Mrs. Min. All one as if you had been in London?

Sir

Sir H. The very fame thing.

Clack. And pray, your honour, what news is ftirring in France?

Sir H. *Toujours* gay, as they fay, Mrs. Clack.

Clack. I reckon there be powers of our country folks there.

Sir H. I fuppofe fo; for I faw a good many aukward people, as they fay, *a la bowlivards*, and at the Coloffus; but I chofe to avoid them.

Min. Why fo? I fhould have been ready to leap out of my fkin at the fight of a countryman in foreign parts.

Sir H. Like enough, Matthew; but you are a *burgois*, as you know; but the Doctor fays, that *un humm de quality*, when he voyages, ought to fhun *les Anglois*.

Clack. I hope you left the royal family all in good health.

Sir H. Yes; Mr. *le Roi*, as the French fay, looked pretty jolly and well; I faw him in one of the glafs-cafes at church, and was afterwards at his grand *couvert*, as they call it; his majefty looked at me very hard: Domine thinks he was ftruck with my figure.

Viper. I overheard him whifper as much to the Duke de Tremouille.

Clack. How long was your honour coming from Paris?

Sir H. Two days and a night.

Clack. Are the accommodations good on the road?

Sir H. Their *chevauxes*, their horfes, as the French call 'em, arn't quite fo nimble as our'n; but then, to make amends, like the French, I *cowrir* the poft without ftopping; unlefs, indeed, to take a flight *repas* of *jambunn* or a *hamlet.*

Clack. The country's vaft pleafant, I reckon.

Sir H. La-la: Their country-folks, their *pheafants*, as the French call 'em, don't feem quite fo tidy as our'n: but they don't look upon them there creatures in France; mere hogs, *cowfhcns*, as they fay.

Mrs. Min. Why, fure they be Chriftians, as well as——

Sir H. Chriftians? why, fo may all the world, if they like it; but it a'n't in every body's power to be a gentleman born: Hey, Domine Viper?

Viper. True, true, Sir Harry. The laws of fubordination are too much neglected in England; all is mere anarchy there; it muft be owned, France is the only fpot for a gentleman.

Sir H. True. Why, a gentleman born may kill a common fellow in Paris, for lefs money than it would coft an unqualified man in England to fhoot a hare or a partridge.

Viper. Right, Baronet: Poor rogues are fo

plenty

plenty in Paris, there is no danger of deſtroying the game.

Sir H. Well ſaid, Domine Viper!—But, Madam Clack, what makes all your family here? Like me, come over to be poliſh'd, I reckon.

Min. Not we; we be contented, Sir Harry, to rub on in our ruſt. You remember our daughter Jenny?

Sir H. Vaſtly well; and ſhe promis'd to turn out a deviliſh fine girl!

Min. Pretty well, as to that.

Sir H. What, I ſuppoſe you have brought her here, juſt to faſhion her; give her the *gout.*

Min. No, no; 'tis a freak of her own: Run away with our 'prentice, to avoid neighbour Codling.

Sir H. A girl of ſpirit, however!

Enter La Jeuneſſe.

La Jeu. Monſieur, on a ſervie.

Sir H. What does he ſay, Domine Viper?

Viper. The dinner's on the table, Sir Harry.

Sir H. Oh, oh!—Domine! it wou'dn't be decent, as them there people are but tradesfolks, you know, to aſk them to dinner?

Viper. Why, yes, you may venture, Sir Harry:

Harry : It is not minded in London; and this town is little better than an Englifh colony.

Sir H. True, true.—Come, good people; as we are all country folks, fuppofe we fit down to table together ?

Min. By all manner of means.

Sir H. Domine, you will efcort Mrs. Min-nikin ? Mrs. Clack, will you accept of my *brafs ?*   [*Exeunt.*

A C T

A C T   II.

[*The fame in* the Trip to Calais, *to* p. 43, *where
O'Donnovan's fpeech was altered, and the fcene
. finifhed, in the following manner.*]

O'Don. So now, as I was a-telling, if you
can get any frind to fpeak to the governor,
why, if they take it into their heads to reftore
her to you, you may chance to have your daughter again.

Min. True, reverend Sir. But, before we
trouble any body, we will firft try what we can
do at the convent ourfelves.

O'Don. By all mains. And, d'ye hear, you
need not mention any thing about the purfe;
you underftand me?

Clack. Your reverence need not fear us.

O'Don. Nay, it is upon account of yourfelves
that I fpeak; becaafe one's charity fhould be private, you know; therefore, to make publication
would take away moft of the merit. If you
fail, I will ftep to the convent, and fee what
can be done.

Mrs. Min. Very kind, reverend Sir. Then,
we will go after the girl to the convent directly.

Clack.

Clack. But take care what you fay! you fee what a hobble we had like to have got into.

Mrs. Min. Never fear; I know how to behave myfelf. [*Exeunt.*

O'Don. It was an odd freak of St. Francis to forbid us touching of money; unlefs, indeed, his firft followers were a parcel of pickpockets, and he thought of this method to break them. But, however, as the hereticks are gone, and there is no danger of giving offince, by St. Francis's lave I will examine the contents of this purfe. Stay! who have we here?

[*Draws back.*

Enter Viper.

Viper. The wind is veering, and when it comes fair, my old knight within will be for hying homewards by the very firft fhip. Let me fee: Can I hit on no fcheme to give him one little fqueeze more? To be fure, what with tailors, *traiteurs*, toymen, the girl, and the gaming-table, my trip to Paris has turn'd out pretty well. One fmart parting blow I fhould be glad to——

O'Don. Save you, good Sir!

Viper. Damn thefe bare-footed beggars! a fet of lazy, lubberly—You may as well fhift your ground, father; you will get nothing from me.

O'Don.

O'Don. Be it ever fo little! we have no-thing but the benevolence of good Chriftian peo—Hey! fure it can't be! by my fhoul, but it is!—What, Doctor Viper! who expected to fee you at Calais?

Viper. Pray, honeft friend, when did our ac-quaintance commence?

O'Don. It is not a very long ftanding. Come, do fhake your memory a bit, Doctor, and you will foon recollect me.

Viper. It will be to no purpofe.

O'Don. I warrant. Surely, my dear, when you were the doer of the Scandalous Chronicle, was not I death-hunter to the very fame paper?

Viper. Hey! why, you can't be Phelim O'Flam!

O'Don. Not now; but I was about twilve months ago.

Viper. What could induce you to turn Ca-puchin?

O'Don. A few murders.

Viper. Murders?

O'Don. Yes; in order to pay off my lodging, I kill'd a couple of dozen of people, that hap-pen'd to be alive and in good health; fo the printer would employ me no longer.

Viper. I told you, O'Flam, what would hap-pen; why, you became a perfect Drawcanfir;

put

put more people to death than any three phyfi-
cians in London.

O'Don. What then, Doctor Viper ? fure,
your poifonous pen did more mifchief than me :
My dead men walk'd about afterwards, and did
their bufinefs as if nothing had happen'd ; whilft
the ftabs made on peoples' good names, by
your rancour and malice, will admit of no confolation.

Viper. How is this ?

O'Don. In fhort, my dear Doctor, the only
difference between us is this ; my dead men are
all alive, and your live men had much better be
dead.

Viper. Do you know, firrah, to whom you are
fpeaking ?

O'Don. You may fay that ; from the top to
the bottom, every chink and cranny, my dear.

Viper. Pay then proper refpect to my cloth.

O'Don. What, d'ye mane it is a prieft that
you are ?

Viper. Without doubt.

O'Don. Then, upon my fhoul, it muft be of
your own ordination, like Mr. Melchizedeck.
A prieft ? I'll wager my frock againft the price
of a mafs, that you can't tell how many the
thirty-nine articles are.

Q   *Viper.*

Viper. An impudent, audacious——

O'Don. A prieſt? What, becaaſe you was' pariſh-clerk to the Moravian meeting-houſe in the Old-Jewry, and us'd to ſnuffle out their bawdy hymns to the tune of beaſtly ballads and jiggs? from thence you got expell'd for robbing the poors' box——

Viper. Me?

O'Don. Then you became advertiſement-ſticker to lottery-offices, auctioneers, ſtage-coaches, and mountebank-doctors; but being detected in ſelling the bills for waſte paper to grocers, you got your diſmiſſal, you know——

Viper. Raſcal! I know?

O'Don. After that you turn'd ſwindler, and got out of gaol by an act for the relief of inſolvent debtors.

Viper. Many honeſt men have been in the ſame ſituation.

O'Don. Lave honeſty out, if you plaaſe. Then you became doer of the Scandalous Chronicle; mow'd down reputations like muck; puſh'd yourſelf into the pay of laJy Deborah Dripping, produced anonymous paragraphs againſt her of your own compoſition, and got paid by her for not putting them into your paper.

Viper.

Viper. Where the devil could the fellow col-lect all this ftory?

O'Don. Now from here, I fuppofe, you will foon return home as a fugitive, and pay your old debts by a new act of parliament.

Viper. Well but, Mr. O'Flam——

O'Don. O' Donnovan, if you plaafe. So you fee, Doctor Viper, you are pretty well known; and all your friends and acquaintance fhall foon know you as well as me in this town.

Viper. The devil! well, but, my dear friend, what can be the meaning of this? why fhould we two quarrel?

O'Don. Whofe fault was it, Doctor, I pray?

Viper. Fault? nobody's fault: I was a little forgetful; that is all. What! we have been connected before; and why fhou'dn't we now? ours is a natural alliance; we are poor dogs, and rich men are our game.

O'Don. For the matter of that, I have no objection to hunting in couples.

Viper. That is right. Come, let us in, and drown all animofity in a bottle of Burgundy.

O'Don. I will wait upon you at night; but I have a little bit of bufinefs at prefent.

Viper. Of what kind?

O'Don. To get a girl out of a convent, and re-ftore her to her frinds and relations.

Q 2   *Viper.*

Viper. A girl?

O'Don. Ay, the daughter of them there Eng=lish within.

Viper. Is the girl handfome?

O'Don. I don't know that, but fhe's young.

Viper. That will go a good way. And fled from her friends?

O'Don. With a lover, they fay.

Viper. Gad, a thought is juft pop'd into my head, that, I fancy, will yield us both a good deal of profit.

O'Don. Of what kind?

Viper. I will inform you within. But where were you bound?

O'Don. To the convent.

Viper. Sufpend your vifit a while. Come with me; I muft introduce you to a friend of mine in the houfe. But, I hope this greafy garb has not tainted your mind with any coy-nefs or qualms.

O'Don. Not a bit; it is a convanient drefs when one can't get any other: It fuits well with the cold of a winter diftrefs; but when the fun and fummer of plenty returns, I fhall fhed my coat like a colt.

" When the devil was ill, the devil a monk would be;
" When the devil was well, the devil a monk was he." [*Exeunt.*
[*The*

[*The fcenes at the Convent fucceeded, as in* the
Trip to Calais; *and the Act ended with no other
variation than the following fmall alteration in
Mrs. Clack's fpeech, p. 52. The Third Act
was all new.*]

Clack. True, fifter. But come; let us go
to THE GOVERNOR, as the friar advifed us; perhaps HE may put us in a way.

ACT

A C T III.

O'Donnovan, Sir Harry Hamper, and Viper, at a table with wine and glasses.

Viper.

WHAT, then, you know her, Sir Harry?

Sir H. From a child; and a sweet little rose-bud she was! by this time, she is in full bloom, no doubt.

Viper. You seem to express yourself with some ardor and warmth, as if you felt a fancy for this fine delicate flower.

Sir H. Pho, pho! what chance have I to get the possession?

Viper. I don't know that; a little contrivance, and the help of a friend, have brought more unlikely matters to bear.

Sir H. Why, Domine, if you would lend your assistance, there might be some hopes, I confess.

Viper. Of me, Sir Harry, you are always secure: But in my old friend here, you will find a more able assistant.

O'Don. You are plaased to compliment, dear Doctor Viper. Unless you are greatly fallen

off,

off, for turning bachelors into hufbands, hufbands into cuckolds, and maids into miftreffes,
there was not a better practitioner within the
bills of mortality.

Viper. My dear monk, a truce to your com-
pliments.

O'Don. Oh, the divil a bit of a compliment!

Viper. Well, well, you are always too kind
to your friends: But, upon this occafion, your
knowledge of this country——

O'Don. That, indade——

Viper. And, above all, the virtues of that
frock, will ftand us in excellent ftead.

O'Den. Why, to fay truth, I know but little
elfe it is good for.

Viper. Well, fhall we have its affiftance?

O'Don. You may fay that.

Viper. If this fcheme fucceeds, knight, it
will do you immortal honour in England;
your intrigue at Paris was a fine preparation.

Sir H. Do you think that is generally known?

Viper. In the mouth of every mortal.

Sir H. Ay? that is lucky indeed! But how
fhall we bring this bufinefs about?

Viper. Nothing fo eafy. Flam is, you know,
defired by the family, if they can't fucceed themfelves, to get the girl out of the convent.

Sir H. True.

Viper.

Viper. That defign is a fufficient pretence for vifiting the girl.

Sir H. Can't be a better.

Viper. As there is little probability that he fhould prevail with Mifs to return to her father and mother, let him pretend to have had an interview with the young fellow her favourite; who lies concealed in the town.

Sir H. Well?

Viper. That, moved to compaffion by their tender attachment, he is determined to lend his aid to accomplifh his wifhes.

O'Don. By this mains, a little fpill will be gained from that quarter too [*afide*].—Has fhe the fhiners, d'ye think?

Viper. I warrant fhe is not come here unprovided. That he is ready to conduct her where her lover lies hid, and lend his miniftry to finifh his bufinefs.

O'Don. I am but a lay-brother, you know.

Viper. Nor I neither: But, for all that, I wouldn't fcruple to tack together twenty couple a-day.

Sir H. I don't doubt it.

O'Don. That, to be fure, is an anfwer.

Sir H. But how does all this concern me?

Viper. I was coming to that. When the monk has got poffeffion of Mifs, what prevents

him

him from bringing the girl to my lodging? where, inftead of her fwain, fhe will be agreeably furprized to encounter Sir Harry.

Sir H. It is a very fine plot, to be fure: But, Domine, fuppofe the young thing fhould be fkittifh, and not quite approve of the change?

Viper. We muft leave you to fettle that bufinefs.; but, from your drefs and addrefs——

O'Don. In trot, fhe muft be more than woman, to refufe fuch a figure.

Viper. A few prefents in hand, and vaft promifes upon returning to England——

Sir H. And you think fhe will comply?

O'Don. Oh, never faar; fhe will melt in a moment.

Viper. Befides, at worft, Flam and I fhall be near you; and if a little compulfion fhould be required——

O'Don. Is it a rape that you main? upon my fhoul, Doctor Viper, you are after ftepping before me a good daal in mifchief.

Viper. A rape! no, no; nothing like it, dear Flam; only a little compulfion, to give the lady an apology for following her own inclinations. Hey, Sir Harry! what are your fentiments upon the occafion?

Sir H. Should like it of all things in the world! I am quite agog, 'till I—How pretty

R   it it will be, to fee the poor thing pout, and fnivel, and fob, and pat me, and cry I warrant, " Go, you naughty thing!"—But is not there fome danger? won't their magiftrates, their policy, as they call it here, take it amifs?

Viper. Oh, no; a gentleman here does whatever he pleafes: Befides, it is but a ftep crofs the Channel, and there, you know, we are fafe.

Sir H. True, true.

Viper. And, upon fecond thoughts, let things turn out as they will, I think it will be right, at your time of life, to report it a rape; it will do your vivacity and vigour a good deal of credit.

Sir H. Will it?

Viper. To be fure. A rape, and upon a nun too, for fo we muft call her; it will fhew a noble contempt for decency, religion, and virtue, and can't fail recommending you to all people of fpirit.

Sir H. I fhould think fo: How one improves by one's travels! Why, this would never have come into my head, had I ftay'd in the city.

Viper. Oh, fy! never; that air is too foggy.

Sir H. I ufed to be a little factious now and then; but that! Lord, that's nothing at all!

Viper. Oh, no merit in that; the natural confequence of your food and your fuel.

Sir

Sir H. But you will take care to paragraph me well in the papers; for if it ſhould not be known, why——

Viper. The main point will be loſt. Never fear! in my old paper, I ſtill keep a place open: That no time may be loſt, I will ſend it to-night.

Sir H. I can't help laughing, to think how my old friends, in Portſoken and Dowgate, will ſtare when they comes to the article.

Viper. Ready to burſt with envy, I warrant!— Well, O'Flam, you know your part; ſet off as ſoon as you pleaſe.

O'Don. Upon my ſhoul, Doctor Viper, there are a few ſcruples and qualms that begin to riſe in my ſtomach.

Viper. Zounds, man, gulp 'em down then as faſt as you can!

O'Don. Upon my conſcience, they won't go; they ſtick ſtill in my troat.

Viper. Hark'ee, Flam! Would not a little *aurum potabile*, a ſmall decoction of guineas, re-move the obſtruction?

O'Don. Why, to daal freely, Doctor, I look upon it there is ſome ſmall danger in what we are about. Now, as to you two, you are but birds of paſſage, you know; and being well winged, can take your flight whenever you plaaſe.

Viper. Well?

O'Don. Now, as to myfelf, tho' I am at home here, yet for all that I am but a ftranger; and being, befides, as bare as a board, it is but raafonable that Sir Harry fhould fpare me fome of his feathers, that may, in cafe of need, carry me out of gun-fhot, you know.

Sir H. By all manner of means.

Viper. But how fhall we manage it? The rules of your order are fo very fevere as to money! I believe I had better receive it; and, if you fhould want——

O'Don. No, no, Doctor; you are a good cafuift, and have filenced moft of my fcruples: Befides, at confeffion tomorrow, it is but lump-ing in this with my other tranfgreffions.

Viper. Sir Harry?

Sir H. Oh, by all manner of means; here!

Viper. Throw it into his cowl.

O'Don. No, no; I can conceal it very well in my fleeve —He might have knocked againft the other, perhaps; and that would not have been altogether fo dacent.

Viper. Well, well; all obftacles being removed, difpatch, my dear Flam, as foon as you can.

O'Don. I fha'n't neglect them. I muft go to vefpers.—But, Doctor Viper, as you are a con-fcientious man, and one of the cloth, don't you
think

think it would be right to have a few prayers put up, for certain perfons, who have in agitation fome important affairs ?

Viper. Why, it mayn't be amifs.

O'Don. The community, you know, is always confidered upon thefe occafions.

Viper. Oh, I dare fay Sir Harry won't fcruple.

Sir H. Not in the leaft. But, to fay truth, the reverend father has drawn me dry for the prefent.

Viper. Oh, you may be foon fupplied in the houfe. Come, I will advance : Here, here !

O'Don. And in paffing by the trunk for the poor, if I was to drop in fomething handfome, you know it might draw down a bleffing upon our defign.

Sir H. Domine, give him the whole purfe !

O'Don. I fhall have great pleafure in farving fo pious a man. Save you, gentlemen ! [*Exit.*

Sir H. A fhrewd fenfible fellow this O'Flam, let me tell you.

Viper. Yes, yes ; he knows what he's about.

Sir H. But, Domine, after the bufinefs is finifh'd, how fhall we difpofe of the girl ?

Viper. Reftore her to her friends, and make it a merit.

Sir H. But if fhe fhould turn out coy, and complain of ill ufage ?

Viper.

Viper. We muſt impute it to ſpite, as by your means ſhe is deprived of her lover.

Sir H. That, indeed—But will they believe it?

Viper. Believe it! Flam and I will ſwear to the faƈt.

Sir H. That indeed—But who have we here?

Enter Mr. and Mrs. Minnikin and Mrs. Clack.

Oh, Mrs. Clack! what ſucceſs have you had?

Clack. Came away juſt as we went; the young jade whines about faſting and penance like a Methodiſt teacher, and talks of embracing poverty, as if ſhe was a peer of the realm.

Min. She poverty? 'tis all a pretence! it is ſomebody elſe ſhe wants to embrace.

Sir H. Why, Domine and I have been laying our noddles together.

Clack. Your worſhip is wonderfully kind!

Viper. Sir Harry has employed a prieſt here in this town; perhaps you have ſeen him?

Mrs. Min. D'ye mean his reverence with the long beard?

Viper. The ſame. The friar is juſt diſpatch'd to the convent; and as the great point is to get the girl out of their clutches, he is to perſuade her that ſhe is to be conduƈted directly to Drugget.

Mrs. Min. But, inſtead of that, he is to bring her to us?

Viper.

Viper. No, no; that would be too abrupt! to Sir Harry Hamper; who, as a friend to the family, will teach her her duty, and what she owes to her friends.

Clack. That will be very kind in his honour.

Sir H. I shall spare no means, Mrs. Clack, to make her submit.

Mrs. Min. But I hope his honour won't push things to extremities; for you know, Matthew, she still is our child.

Min. Extremities! Sir Harry has undertaken a more difficult task than he is aware of: The young slut is so headstrong and fractious, that my old friend will find it out of his power, if she continues obstinate, to make her comply.

Sir H. Well, well; it is but trying, however.

Viper. You will take care to be in the house if we should want you. Come, Sir Harry, we must hie home, to wait for the monk.

[*Exeunt Sir Harry and Viper.*

Clack. Come, good folks, who can tell but his honour may compass this job?

Min. I can't say I have any great expectations. My old friend, when he liv'd amongst us, was never over-famous for his powers of persuasion; and I can hardly think that age has improv'd his abilities. [*Exeunt.*

The

The Street.

Enter Dick Drugget.

Dick. It is impoffible for me to quit this town, and leave my deareft Jenny behind me; there my heart's treafure lies hid, and there, fpite of myfelf, I am carried by an irrefiftible impulfe. To fee her, I fuppofe, is impoffible; and equally difficult to give or receive any intelligence. Hufh! I muft hide.—Hey! no, fure! yes; it is Jenny her-felf! but who the deuce can it be that conducts her?

Enter O' Donnovan and Jenny.

O'Don. The houfe is hard-by, at the other end of the town; and ftands alone, between the inn and the fnuff-fhop.

Jenny. Your goodnefs, my dear father, to a poor unfortunate victim, I want words to acknowledge. Your felf-denial and mortified ftate place you above the reach of any pecu-niary——

O'Don. My fweet pretty cratur! in acts of charity, indade, to folks poorer than we are, if any fuch can be found, we are always plaas'd to convey any donations.

Jenny. I fhall think myfelf happy to affift fo pious a purpofe [*feels for her purfe*].—Blefs me!

is

is not that my dear Dicky, who ſtands there at the corner?

O'Dcn. Dear Dicky! who the divil is he?

Jenny. The very youth to whom you were going to convey me.

O'Don. Pho, pho! how can that be? be-caaſe why, I left him at home; and how can he be in two places at once? unleſs, indade, he had wings.

Jenny. His impatience, I ſuppoſe, made him follow you hither.

O'Don. Pox take his impatience! But I tell you, Miſs, it can't be; becaaſe why, I never ſaw that parſon before.

Jenny. But I have, and therefore can't doubt: I muſt run to him, father; for I know it is he.

O'Don. Is it? Then my beſt way is to run from him as faſt as I can. [*Exit.*

Jenny. Dicky!

Dick. My deareſt Jenny! this is an unex-pected pleaſure indeed. But who was that with you?

Jenny. The honeſt father you ſent to con-duct me.

Dick. Me? I have neither ſeen nor ſpoke to a ſoul.

Jenny. No!

S   *Dick.*

Dick. No. This is some plot of your parents, to get you into their clutches.

Jenny. Perhaps so. But where can we go? have you secur'd no retreat?

Dick. How could I, my love? as I hadn't the smallest hopes of—But here comes the priest again, and somebody with him; let us turn down this street, and avoid him.   [*Exeunt.*

Enter O'Donnovan and Viper.

O'Don. There, there they go!

Viper. I see, I see. A fine girl, as I live! too nice a tid-bit for an apprentice, or my musty old knight: I'll try if I can't secure her myself.—O'Flam! you know Bet Bonnet, the milliner's girl, that lived with me in London?

O'Don. You may say that.

Viper. When I went with the knight, I left her in my lodgings in town; step to her this instant.

O'Don. Well?

Viper. Explain to her the business of Hamper, convey her to him as Minnikin's daughter; she knows well enough how to assume the airs of a novice.—But there is hardly time to instruct her. Ten to one, too, this blockhead

will

will make fome damn'd blunder or other.—
O'Flam!

O'Don. Well?

Viper. Upon fecond thoughts, you had beft
undertake this bufinefs yourfelf.

O'Don. What d'ye main?

Viper. Pais yourfelf on the knight as the
party.

O'Don. What, me, for old Minnikin's
daughter?

Viper. Ay.

O'Don. Oh, lave off! I fhall be aafily taken
for a lovely lafs, to be fure.

Viper. Why not? he muft be in the dark, to
execute his own intentions, you know.

O'Don. That is true. But how fhall I hide
my voice? he may fee that, you know, without
the help of a candle; befides, I am told I have
a fmall twift in my tongue.

Viper. Oh, as to that, Hamper is no critic in
dialects; befides, fay little, and foften your
tones as much as you can.

O'Don. But if he fhould turn out too familiar, what will I do then, Doctor Viper?

Viper. It will be eafy enough to repel any
violence from a man of his age. Befides, I
will think of fome expedient to bring you
fpeedy relief.

O'Don.

O'Don. Well, well! upon my fhoul, after all, there is a good daal of fun in the fancy.

Viper. You are to take him for Drugget, you know,

O'Don. No bad match for my linfey-woolfey.

Viper. Oh, a truce to your wit now, and difpatch, I befeech you.

O'Don. I go, I go.   [*Exit.*

Viper. They are either houfed, or muft return back again; this is no thoroughfare. Oh, here they come.

Enter Dicky and Jenny.

I am glad I have met with you. Come, come! I hav'n't a moment to lofe.

Jenny and Dicky. Sir!

Viper. That rafcally prieft is gone for the guard; you will have a file of mufqueteers here in a minute.

Dicky. What have I done?

Viper. Done! don't you know, that to fteal a girl from a convent in this country is a capital crime?

Dicky. Sir, as I hope for mercy, I am innocent!

Viper. Innocent! befides, a prieft to accufe you! won't they find you together? is not that proof enough of your guilt? In a word, I know
your

your whole ſtory; I pity, and am ready to ſerve you.

Jenny. Good Sir, what can we do?

Viper. You hav'n't a moment to loſe: Run to the port, throw yourſelf into the firſt veſſel you ſee, and make for England as faſt as you can.

Dicky. And what muſt become of Miſs Jenny?

Viper. Leave her to my care; I am well known in this town, and can conceal her with eaſe.

Jenny. But, Sir, how—who——

Viper. Oh, child, be under no apprehenſions; my motive is ſolely compaſſion: Beſides, my cloth is a ſufficient ſecurity.

Dicky. Cloth? perhaps the gentleman is a clergym——

Viper. Huſh! that muſt not be known where we are.

Jenny. On that ſacred character I can ſafely rely.

Viper. We loſe time! a truce to your regrets, and your raptures; I will ſoon bring you to-gether, I warrant. That way leads to the quay. Come, Miſs; it is but a ſtep to my houſe.

Jenny. This wonderful eſcape I owe to your goodneſs.

Viper. I could do no leſs, as a Chriſtian. [*Exe.*

A Chamber,

A Chamber, darkened.

Sir Harry Hamper alone.

Sir H. Mifs will foon be here, I fuppofe. Well, after all, for improving the mind, and removing foolifh prejudices, there is no country like France : No wonder our young folks of fafhion turn out fuch fine fellows, ecod!— Here fhe is, I believe. No.—A lad who comes over here at nineteen or twenty, may well pick up all the pretty accomplifhments, when I, at feventy, in lefs than three months, have learnt to game, whore, defpife my own country, laugh at religion, and, as far as inclination will go, am ripe and ready for any frolic or fun. Well faid, old Harry! After all this, my young miftrefs in London can't refufe me, I think; the devil's in her, if I hav'n't done enough to convince her that I have fcowered off all the fneaking fniveling cit, and am as profligate as if I had been born a— Hufh! the door opens.

Enter O' Donnovan.

O'Don. Sir Harry !

Sir H. Well ?

O'Don. Are you fure you are there ?

Sir H. Without doubt.

O'Don.

O'Don. And alone?

Sir H. Yes.

O'Don. And no light?

Sir H. Don't you fee?

O'Don. I didn't know but you might have a candle concaaled.

Sir H. Where? in my pocket?

O'Don. Come, Mifs, you may enter. [*Exit.*

Jenny [*within*]. Hands off, you rude ruffian!

Sir H. What the deuce noife are they making?

Jenny. What, are they all dead in the houfe? no creature to lend me affiftance?

Sir H. What can this mean?

Jenny. Or have you all confpired to betray me? For Heaven's fake, fome Chriftian body——

Mrs. Min. [*within.*] It is my daughter's voice. Here, houfe!

Min. [*within.*] Zounds, break down the door!

Mrs. Min. Which room are they in?

Min. The noife came from this.

Enter Mr. and Mrs. Minnikin, Mrs. Clack, Colonel, O'Donnovan, and Codling.

Min. Have you feen any thing of my daughter, Sir Harry?

Sir H. Your daughter!

Jenny. Unhand me! This door too is locked. What, will no mortal come to me?

Mrs.

Mrs. Min. There fhe is.

Min. Let me come!   [*Breaks open the door.*

Enter Jenny.

Jenny. Protect me, fave me——

Mrs. Min. It is her. Look up, Jenny! don't you know us, my child ?

Jenny. My mother ? Oh, Madam !

Mrs. Min. Recover your fright ; you are now out of danger. What has been the matter, my love ?

Jenny. The greateft villain, the greateft monfter!

Min. Who ? what ?

Jenny. Firft got me into his power, by the pretended fanctity of his character——

Min. Well ?

Jenny. Finding his delufive offers rejected, proceeded to violence, when my cries brought you to my aid.

Min. This is fome *parle vou* rafcal ! they don't mind a rape or a robbery here.

Mrs. Min. Not they ; Lord fend us fafe to Old England, fay I !

Min. Come out here ! let us have a peep at your muns, Mounfeer, if you pleafe. [*Pulls out Viper.*] Hey ! who the devil——Why, this is Sir Harry's Domine Viper !

Omnes. Sure enough !

Min.

Min. His tuterer, as fure as a gun! But who the deuce is he, Sir Harry?

Sir H. Heaven knows! I pick'd him up here in this town.

Mrs. Min. Some vagaboning feller, I warrant.

Min. The rafcal won't make a reply. Come, friend! who and what are you?

Viper. What right have you to enquire?

Min. Your villainous attack on my daughter gives me a right; and before we part I will know.

Viper. Will you? Then afk it of thofe that will tell you.

Min. What, can nobody——

Clack. Perhaps his reverence here may; for he feems to know moft of the folks in the town.

O'Don. Me? I know nobody, out of the convent.—I belaave I had better fhaar off; for perhaps by-and-bye they may take it into their heads to make fome enquiries after me of myfelf; and, for the prefent, it will be more convanient to drop the acquaintance. [*Exit.*

Min. But, what the deuce, can nobody give us an account who he is? Where's landlord?

Colonel. You feem all ftrangers to this honeft gentleman.

Min. Oh, this perhaps is fomebody who belongs to the town. Why, Sir, if you could give us fome information——

T

Colonel.

Colonel. Nay, I can't boaft the honour of his acquaintance, nor; from the account of his countrymen, fhould I be very ambitious to make it.

Min. Ay, like enough ; and pray, Sir, who—

Colonel. The various particulars of his hiftory would be rather too tedious at prefent : thus far I may venture to fay ; his refidence here is not a mere matter of choice.

Viper. Is the preferring the genial climate of France, to the fogs of your favourite ifle, any great matter of wonder ? In fhort, I like neither your country nor people.

Colonel. For which you have doubtlefs very good reafons : But believe this as a truth, Mafter Viper ; no man ever yet deferted his country, unlefs he had been firft by his country deferted.

Viper. You are very partial, Colonel (for I know you), confidering England as a fpot to which you can never lay any claim.

Colonel. Why not?

Viper. Wafn't your father a rebel ?

Colonel. True.

Viper. And are not you an officer in the fervice of France ?

Colonel. I was ; but my prefent royal mafter, above the narrow prejudice of punifhing the principles of parents in their unfortunate offspring,

fpring, has accepted my fervice, and reftored my family to the rights of their country.

Clack. Well faid!

Sir H. Ay, and well done too! to reclaim by clemency, is the nobleft victory a monarch can gain over his fubjects.

Min. But what can we do with this fellow? is there no method of punifhing fuch a——

Colonel. Let him alone; a gentleman of his particular turn can't long efcape the prying eyes of the police in this town; and I promife you they fhan't want a key to his character.

Sir H. But, Colonel, I begin to fufpect that I too have been bit by this Viper; couldn't I ftop him, juft to make him account for——

Viper. Stop me? you had beft take care of yourfelf: You forget a few obligations of yours I have in my pocket; which, as I find you are quitting this country, I fhall endeavour to get better fecured.   [*Exit.*

Sir H. Now there is a rafcal!

Colonel. How came you to place any confidence in a man without the fmalleft recommendation?

Sir H. Lord, who could fuppofe that a countryman would impofe upon——

Colonel. Your countrymen? the very laft

people, unlefs they are well known, you fhould
truft or cherifh in France.

Sir H. And why fo?

Colonel. The neceffity they lie under of fhift-
ing their quarters, is, with but too many
of them, their only reafon for croffing the
Channel.

Min. Indeed?

Colonel. And I will venture to fay, without
the concurrence of fome of thefe gentry, no
confiderable fraud has ever been committed upon
our young giddy travellers in this part of the
world.

Codl. Vaft curus indeed! that fhall go into
my journal. "Obferwation: The French who
" rob and cheat the Britifh fubjects in Paris,
" are all of them Englifh."

Mrs. Min. Ay, ay; all birds of a feather.
Let us go home and leave them, as faft as we
can. Well, Jenny, I hope there is an end of
all thy vagaries: Thee feeft what premunirers
thy wilfulnefs had near brought us into.

Clack. Nay, fifter, don't prefs the girl for
the prefent: Let Mr. Codling continue his
courtfhip; and in time, I warrant, the girl will
comply.

Codl. Why, father-in-law that was to have
been,

been, it feems to me, and to fay truth, from the famples I have had, before I fettles I fhould like to fee a little more of the world.

Min. Nay, Mafter Codling, you may do as you lift; nobody wants to compel you.

Mrs. Min. For the matter of that, if Dick Drugget's friends are inclined, they are well to pafs in the world; and who can tell, in the end, but one match may be as good as the other?

Codl. Why, as they are fo vaft fond of each other, I think it is the beft ftep you can take. For my part, I have made up my mind: I'll part with my fhop, voyage round the world for the reft of my life, and, like other great travellers, communicate my obferwations, for the good of my country.

F I N I S,